A WAGER WITH A DUKE

TAMARA

COPYRIGHT

A WAGER WITH A DUKE, The Wayward Yorks, Book 1 ©
2023 by Tamara Gill
Cover Art by Wicked Smart Designs
Editor Grace Bradley Editing, LLC

ISBN: 978-0-6457488-5-7 (trade paperback)

ONE

Henry strolled through Whites and, with a sporadic glance down at the betting book, halted his steps in an instant. Normally, what was scribbled in the tome would not seize his attention. He wasn't in London to rut about like so many others were wont to do. But the sight of the new-to-town Miss Sophie York's name, in bold black font and forthright on the page, caught his engagement.

Although she had not been deemed the Season's diamond due to her lack of fortune, this year's favorite was part of a bet. He shook his head, having lost count of how many ladies were termed such. Who really knew who was the most accomplished, well-bred, pretty, and pure? If those were all the requirements for being the

1

most sought-after in London, then he could qualify.

A large hand slapped his back and lurched him forward. He tumbled toward the betting book before he righted his stance.

"Holland, are you going to add your name to the bet? Come, man, we know you'll likely win if you do. Not a woman in London who could refuse your charm, or so I'm told on a nightly basis," Lord Bankes affirmed at his side. A notion that many in London and, in fact, across England were led to believe.

Not that any of it was true. If the *ton* knew of his sexual inexperience, he would be laughed out of London by nightfall.

"Perchance I shall," he said, picking up the quill and scribbling his name below so many others. He did not mind playing along with the illusion. It kept him secure in many ways.

"Miss Sophie York, I must admit, is the purest angel to ever walk the wooden floorboards of London's most affluent homes. I daresay that under her fine gowns—even if they were bestowed upon her by the Countess of Kemsley—hide two deity wings that would carry her up to the heavens themselves."

Henry scoffed and turned his rudeness into a cough. He nodded, not daring to disagree with a man so exemplary with his explanation of the divine.

"I certainly agree. We have not been intro-duced, but I have seen her at different events, and I hope to gain an introduction soon."

"Well, you must if you wish to win this bet. You do know what you scribbled your name down beneath, do you not?" Bankes asked him, his eyes alight with curiosity.

"Of course," Henry stated, his answer brooking no argument. He swallowed and quickly read the terms of the bet and balked.

"Who wrote this bet up? The first gentleman to make her fall in love with him wins a thousand pounds?" He continued reading and felt his eyes growing ever larger by the minute. "To help with her lack of dowry when the nuptials occur."

Henry almost cast up his accounts at what he signed, not that he had to take the bet too seri-ously. He could easily ignore that he ever signed it and pretend to participate.

Another part of him cringed at the idea of Miss York not knowing that she was the center of such a ruse and would not know why so many gentlemen would court her and pay attention to her every desire.

"True, she isn't flush with cash, but if you look at all the names written, they're all rich enough to support her and her mother, whom I hear lives in a cottage in the country somewhere. But," Bankes continued, "she is a pretty little debutante and will make a splendid bed partner. I do hope she's not as angelic in the sheets as she appears on the dance floor. I would appreciate a vixen in the bedroom."

"Indeed," Holland managed, turning on his heel and leaving Bankes at the betting book alone. He was in London to find a wife. He was eight and twenty, old enough to settle and have children, an heir if he were so fortunate, but to court a person without their knowing of the game afoot was wrong.

He hated to think what she would say or how she would react should she become aware that whoever won her heart had played such a game with the gentlemen in town this Season.

Well, he would not do it. He would pretend to take part but not court her, no matter how pretty she was. Plenty of other young women were just as sweet-tempered and new to town whom he could meet.

Not to mention several embarking on their second or even third Season. A wallflower would suit his temperament, his genuine one in any case. He did not like to be the hub of attention, the beau of the ball, the rake every matron wanted in her bed, no matter what anyone else said or thought.

Somehow he had managed to garner a reputation of a rogue by merely being secretive. Which was not mysterious at all, merely introverted. The fact his father passed from syphilis was foremost in his mind whenever the thought occurred to spread his seed recklessly.

He slumped into one of the plush leather chairs Whites sported and waved a footman over. A glass of stiff liquor was just what he needed. The Derby ball was this evening, where the games of courtship and playing the doting gentleman would begin.

He would need all the fortitude of the amber liquid in his hand he could get. There was nothing wrong with liquid courage, after all.

SOPHIE TOOK A DEEP, CALMING BREATH and then placed her hand into that of Lord Kemsley, who helped her alight from the carriage. This evening was the Duke and Duchess of Derby's ball, not the first she had attended this year, but anyone who was anyone in society was rumored to attend. A very select invitation list that she was grateful to be a part of. Not that she could say she was invited under her own merit, she had Harlow and Lord Kemsley and their connections to thank for the honor.

They entered the sizeable Georgian manor on Berkeley Square, waiting like several other attendees to make their addresses to the hosts before entering the ballroom.

Sophie glanced down at her exquisite gown

from Madame Laurent. The gown had been delivered this afternoon, and it was the loveliest dress she had ever owned, nevertheless worn. Made of the lightest shade of yellow, under the candlelight, it shimmered like gold. The dark-green braiding across the bodice and short sleeves only added to its beauty.

Her cousin Harlow was too sweet and kind to her, and she would forever be in her debt for giving her a Season.

She did not deserve one. Not really. Although she smiled and giggled when gentlemen bestowed compliments upon her, it was all a ruse. If only they knew her secret, they would tip their noses far into the air and leave her to herself. Friendless and alone, much as she was before she left Highclere.

"This ball is certain to be exciting for you, Sophie. I see Lord Bankes and Mr. Fairbanks have already spied your attendance," Harlow said after greeting their hosts and entering the ballroom.

Sophie tried not to let the magnificence of the room overwhelm her or make her gape as she was wont to do when rooms as grand as this one were manifested before her.

The wealth in London was beyond anything she had ever known, Harlow not excluded from that. Lord Kemsley doted on her cousin, and there was nothing they wanted for.

There were times in Highclere when she and

her mother accepted every invitation to dine with friends in the small village merely so they could eat well, at least for one night. No one about her would know just how low her family had fallen and what a once-in-a-lifetime gift her cousin was giving by sponsoring her.

She did not know whether or not a nice gentleman would offer his hand in marriage, but she could dream. That she was here was gift enough, and while she did not expect to marry a titled gentleman, she hoped whomever she married, a barrister, solicitor, or doctor, that she would never face hunger again. Never have to fret about how to pay the butcher or coal merchant.

She reached for Harlow's arm and linked hers with her cousin. "I cannot thank you enough for having me here with you. I know my mama's letter sounded quite desperate and—"

"Hush," Harlow said, patting her arm. "There is no need for any more thanks. We're family, and thankfully we get along so very well that I could not think of you leaving or not getting what your heart desires. You deserve only the best, and I'm going to find you a husband who is simply perfect for you."

Sophie hoped that would be so. She looked across the sea of heads and her heart stuttered at the sight of the Duke of Holland. Harlow took note of her interest, her little knowing giggle told Sophie she had also spied the duke.

"Is he not one of the most handsome men in London? Excluding my husband, of course, but he would do splendidly as your spouse. He's un-attached, titled, and wealthy. The perfect three points that I want for you."

Sophie shook her head but could not wipe the smile from her lips at her cousin's expecta-tions. "I do not think he would consider me at all. He's a duke, for heaven's sake, and a rogue, from what I hear. Not that I'm supposed to know this, but I heard Lady Leigh mention at your home the other afternoon that he's having a love affair with a dowager marchioness."

Harlow glanced at her, her eyes wide with mortification. "You should not listen to such con-versations, Sophie. I apologize you heard such things."

Sophie did not mind at all. How was one to find out who would suit her if she did not listen to gossip? She needed a man who would not know the intimate specialties of a woman, espe-cially if a woman had been with a man.

The despair of her disgrace swamped her, and for a moment, she deflated like a flower in the sun too long. A rogue such as the Duke of Holland would know she was not a virgin on their wed-ding night, and he would hate her for it. He would possibly send her from their bedchamber and ask for an annulment. And then she would be ruined, this time, however, publicly.

All she had was the ability to keep her disgrace from becoming known, and she needed a man who was less knowledgeable about women than the opposite.

"It did not offend me at all. It helps me understand which gentlemen are seriously looking for a wife and those who are not. Nothing untoward or lewd was said, I promise. Please do not say anything to Lady Leigh."

"Very well," Harlow said with a sigh. "I will not, but come. I see Lord Bankes looks to be heading our way. I think your first dance is about to take place."

Sophie looked in the direction of the earl. He was less handsome than the Duke of Holland, but he would be a perfect candidate for a husband, she guessed, from the way he fiddled with his cravat and patted down his hair. He did not look like he had ever spoken to a woman, nevertheless slept with one.

She bestowed upon him her sweetest smile, and he all but turned as red as a beet.

The perfect gentleman, indeed.

Two

B y the time the second hour of the ball passed, Sophie's toes ached from the numerous times they were trodden on. Her poor new slippers looked far less pretty than they had been when she arrived at the ball earlier.

Not that she would complain about such trivial matters, even if her toes were bruised the following day. She was dancing, enjoying a ball, thanks to her cousin. She would never have had the opportunity to attend had she not been so fortunate as to know Harlow.

Sophie stood beside a window, cracked open a little to allow the cooling night air to enter, and sipped a glass of lemonade. A moment of peace and respite as Harlow and Lord Kemsley enjoyed a waltz together.

She watched them, pleasure filling her at the love the couple had for each other. She would be a simpleton indeed if she did not strive for such a love, to have a husband who looked at her the way Lord Kemsley gazed at his wife.

How wonderful that would be.

"Miss York, I hope you're enjoying the ball," Mr. Fairbanks said, bowing before her.

She dipped into a curtsy and smiled. "Mr. Fairbanks, how lovely to see you again, and yes indeed, I'm enjoying the ball as I hope you are?" she asked him.

He came and stood beside her, a lofty expression on his handsome visage. "I am enjoying the ball all the more now that I know you are in attendance. The London Season seems to suit you," he said. "You're from the country, are you not?"

"Yes, the small village of Highclere. My mama still resides there," she said, not wanting to explain further about her life. The fewer people that knew of her, the less chance there was of someone finding out that she was not as she appeared.

When people looked at her, they saw innocence, a pretty face even, a woman of little means but with high connections. And she supposed she was all those things, bar one.

She was not innocent.

Sophie drove the unhelpful thought aside and took another sip of her lemonade. "The ball is a crush. I do not believe I've been to such an entertainment this Season where one finds it difficult to move about."

"Yes, the Duke and Duchess of Derby invite all who are worthy, and no one dares refuse, hence the crush. But, at least, it allows for more intimate conversation since we're forced to stand nearer to the other."

The sparking glint of innuendo in Mr. Fairbanks's eye reminded her of Lord Carr and her mistake of thinking all men acted like gentlemen when they did not.

No good came from believing such falsehoods.

She hoped Mr. Fairbanks was honest and kind. All the things he was portraying himself to be, but she was uncertain. The number of gentlemen who paid her calls and danced with her nightly left her reeling and unsure whom to trust and believe at any one moment.

"Her Grace, I suppose, wants to make her ball the most enjoyed and talked about, until the next one. I can see why they invite so many. Should I ever have the luxury of being a hostess on such a grand scale, I would like the same. Do you not think this is simply marvelous?" The ballroom glistened in the candlelight. The women's gowns were a rainbow of colored silks in the room, not to mention the jewels. So many pretty diamonds and other gemstones that Sophie could only covet. How lucky these people were, and most of them would never know how much.

Mr. Fairbanks watched her keenly. What was the man thinking? Did he find her answer in poor taste? She knew the *ton* did not speak of marriage or fine things, but she was neither of those, so did the rules really apply to her?

"You would make a beautiful hostess," he said.

She smiled and glanced across the ballroom floor, needing to close that line of conversation before it became inappropriate. A sizzle ran down her spine at the sight of the Duke of Holland. He stood talking to the Duke and Duchess of Derby, his height and stature pulling any lady's eye in his direction. He was so handsome, so commanding, and aloof.

What a shame she could not win someone so grand as he. But he was far from innocent and would learn her secret and despise her for it.

As if sensing her inspection, he glanced in her direction, and the breath in her lungs seized. Their eyes met and held for one tantalizing moment before he turned back to his friends.

Oh, dear, oh dear, oh dear, he was lovely.

Trouble with a capital T if she were any judge of character.

"That is the Duke of Holland, Miss York. Have you been introduced?" Mr. Fairbanks asked her.

Heat kissed her cheeks that he had noticed her regard for the man, and she shook her head, averting her gaze to anywhere but at the duke, who was too attractive to be fair.

"I do not know many in town. Lady Kemsley, is trying to remedy that, but I believe she will fall short."

Mr. Fairbanks gestured for her to walk with him. "I can introduce you if you like. It would be my pleasure. From what I understand, the duke has not been in London since last Season and only arrived several days ago."

Butterflies fluttered in Sophie's stomach, and she questioned whether it would be in good taste if she allowed Mr. Fairbanks to introduce her to Lord Holland.

She looked around for Harlow and found her in conversation with Lady Jenkins.

Sophie turned to Mr. Fairbanks and slipped her arm through his in agreement. "Very well. I see no harm in being introduced. And since I know the Duke and Duchess of Derby, I see no disadvantage in being polite."

"I could not agree more." Mr. Fairbanks grinned, leading her toward the man who appeared more like a god than a mortal and possibly just as untouchable as those mystical beings.

THE HAIRS ON THE BACK OF HENRY'S neck prickled in awareness, and he reached up and clasped his muscles there. He turned without knowing the reason why and his stomach clenched.

One of the most beautiful women he'd ever seen stood looking up at him. Her large, blue eyes watched him with interest and a little awe, and for a moment, he could not look away.

He met Mr. Fairbanks's laughing gaze and narrowed his eyes on the gentleman, fully aware of his amusement and what he was up to. Reminding him of the bet he'd been foolish enough to put his name to. And all because he could not stomach being outed for the fraud he was.

"The Duke and Duchess of Derby, I believe you know Miss York, but may I introduce Miss York to you, Your Grace?" Mr. Fairbanks said to him. "Miss York, this is the Duke of Holland."

The light-haired goddess with lips made for kissing dipped into a deep curtsy, and he glanced about, not sure it needed to be so regal in depth.

"Your Grace, this is Miss Sophie York from Highclere. She is the cousin of Lady Kemsley," Fairbanks explained.

Henry bowed. "It is a pleasure to meet you, Miss York," he said, unable to tear his gaze from her eyes. They were the darkest blue he had seen in many years. When he had noticed her across the ballroom floor, they had shone like jewels in the candlelight. "I hope you're enjoying your stay in town?" he asked, desiring this conversation to not be awkward. Her large eyes and rose-kissed cheeks told him she was a little flustered, but as to why he could not fathom.

"I am, Your Grace. Thank you for asking."

Henry wracked his brain, searching for more to say, and thankfully the Duchess of Derby came to his rescue.

"I hope you're attending our picnic to-morrow afternoon, Miss York. I know you wished to see our conservatory, and I have ensured it's the prettiest it can be for your visit," the duchess said warmly.

"You enjoy gardening?" Henry asked her. It was a hobby of his, and this was a fortunate turn of events. They may have something to talk about after all.

"I like hothouse flowers, Your Grace. The different scents. I have a little book, a hobby where I try to explain the scent. I'm not very good at it, and these past weeks I have neglected it terribly, but should someone wish for a particular rose, for example, and they would like a particular scented rose, I think this could be a useful resource. Not that I have completed many. I did not have the opportunity in Highclere to study much."

"Your estate did not have a hothouse?" he

asked her and regretted his question immediately when she paled before them all.

"We were not so fortunate, Your Grace."

She did not elaborate, and he met Derby's eyes and knew he had to try to repair the faux pas he had just created between them all.

"Will you dance with me, Miss York?" he blurted before he could think better of it.

Her eyes lost the despair they had formed and she blossomed before him. "I would like that very much, Your Grace. Thank you."

THREE

Sophie steeled herself to be led out onto the dance floor, by a duke no less. Her stomach twisted and turned when he held out his hand. With as much delicacy and perfection as she could muster, she laid her hand atop his and, raising her chin, allowed him to lead her onto the floor.

Several ladies cast startled looks their way, and several gentlemen too. Still, she fought to ignore the noise about her and concentrate on dancing with a gentleman who was as high in society as one could get without being royal.

The realization almost made her cast up her accounts.

She swallowed, took a deep, calming breath, and entered his arms. He was tall, much taller than she first thought upon meeting him. But being so close, feeling the superfine coat beneath her palms and the corded, flexing muscles beneath made her conscious that the gentleman she danced with was a young, virile man.

A very handsome one too.

Sandalwood mixed with a sweet, floral scent bombarded her senses. Did he have it made from the flowers that grew in his hothouse? No doubt, the duke had an array of servants to cater to his every whim.

He swept her into the waltz, and for several minutes she counted and focused on remembering the steps as correctly and perfectly as a debutante should.

Not that she was really a debutante. She was two and twenty, much older than the other young ladies making their debut this year, not to mention she was not as innocent as them either.

She could only hope that her secret, her disgrace, was never found out, or such delightful dances as the one she was having would be no more. To think she could bring embarrassment to her cousin was not what she wanted, not after all Harlow had done for her, and so playing the role of a sweet innocent miss was paramount.

"You're the cousin of Lady Kemsley, and Lady Billington I understand. I know Lord Kemsley well," the duke said, meeting her gaze fleetingly.

She nodded, watching him and marveling at his straight, aristocratic nose and strong jawline. Hunger twisted in her stomach, but not the kind that told her she wanted a repast. Oh no, this hunger was for an entirely different reason and one she ought not to feel. The duke was so far out of her league as to be fanciful. He would not marry a nobody without family or funds. Not to mention everything else she had done to ruin herself.

"They are the best of family," she admitted. "I cannot thank Lady Kemsley enough for all that she has done for me," she said, seeing no reason not to be honest. She was poor and reliant on others for her Season. She would not pretend on that score to be someone whom she was not.

"I apologize if I offended you earlier about your residence. I did not mean to upset you with my question. I forget, you see, that not everyone is the same in this society."

How lovely of him to apologize. It only made Sophie like him even more. "I've never been asked so directly if I were as fortunate as you and others to have a hothouse. But no, we do not, although the now dowager Lady Carr from a nearby estate to Highclere allowed me to use her conservatory when I was not reading to her mother-in-law." A sanctuary for so many years until that fateful evening when she had come across the now-deceased Lord Carr's heir, Baron Saunders, as he was then known. "But now I contend myself with Lady Kemsley's hothouse." She met his eyes and held them. "I'm impoverished, you see, Your Grace. I have no dowry or grand family with connections and wealth. And while I'm grateful that you're dancing with me this evening, I do not want you to think I have designs on you in any way. I know that you're merely being nice."

The duke's mouth gaped before he stuttered out his words of reply. "Miss York, I did not ask you to dance entirely to make amends. I do not do anything that I do not wish to."

"I should hope not," she replied with a laugh, trying to lighten the mood. "I suppose what I'm trying to say is that I will not follow you about for the rest of the Season, my eyes brimming with longing merely because you were kind to me this night."

A small frown line appeared between his brows, and she fought not to swoon at how delicious he was. Truly, the man was beyond handsome. Was he even aware of the effect he had on women? His thick, dark locks made one want to run their fingers through and clasp them tight. She supposed he would know his allure. He was rumored, after all, to be a wild rake who was never without a bed partner.

He probably knew how to kiss well too.

"I should be honored if you were smitten with me, Miss York, but I thank you for your honesty. In fact, I do not think I have ever spoken to any lady during any Season in London who has been as honest as you have been this night. It is much refreshing."

He pulled her into a tight curve and spun them before they started to waltz down the opposite side of the room.

"You're very welcome, Your Grace," she replied, relishing their conversation immensely. "May I ask if you've been enjoying London? I have not seen you at many balls or parties so far."

His fingers flexed on her hip, and she fought not to shiver. He had large hands, strong too, she would imagine. The idea of him picking her up filled her mind, and she almost sighed.

For all her talk of not becoming smitten by him, she would soon be doing that very thing if she did not get her emotions under control. Or her womanly demands.

"I've only recently arrived, but I'm here, and it is time to search for a wife. Not that I would like for you to make that fact known. I do not need the headache of many mamas throwing their daughters before me. I can choose well enough myself."

"Of course, I shall not say a word. My lips are sealed."

His gaze dipped to her mouth, and he stared at her for several heartbeats. The feeling of need was back again, clawing at her, thrumming through her body like a siren's call to be devilish. To throw all that she had worked so hard to suppress, to hide, and allow it to come to the surface.

He cleared his throat and averted his eyes to somewhere over the top of her head. "Thank you. I'm grateful for your assistance with this."

"You're very welcome," she replied, smiling at him and happy to see his lips twitched in return.

HENRY FOUGHT TO KEEP HIS BREATHING regulated. Who was this woman in his arms who made him want to forget about being the righteous, virtuous duke? He was starting to think that being such an honorable gentleman meant that he could not try to seduce this sweet, lovely woman in his arms, and that realization was not ideal.

He studied her, unable to keep himself from doing so. She was tall, but not such a long meg that she met him eye to eye. The perfect height to clasp one's cheeks, lean down, and thoroughly kiss without stooping.

Would she welcome his kiss?

Possibly not this evening since they had just met, but if they became friends ...

He had signed the betting book along with many others, so his interest in her would not cause eyebrows to rise, not among the gentlemen in any case. He never enjoyed ribbing, and his friends would merely think he was trying to make her fall in love with him to win the thousand-pound bet.

A small smile played across her lips, and he watched her. She was so unaware of how beautiful she was. Her words earlier to him were proof of that.

She did not expect anything from him and did not want him to think she had designs on his title.

A knot of annoyance settled in his gut. He did not like her thinking of herself in such a way. Unworthy and beneath him. While financially and socially the disparity of their lives was quite vast, that did not make him above her reach.

Many men as wealthy and titled as he had married women of no rank or fortune. She was not so far beneath him that he would not notice her.

He had noticed her the moment he saw her speaking to Lord Fairbanks across the ballroom floor.

But he also appreciated the freedom she afforded him. Her declaration meant that they could be friends first and foremost. No expectations, no hurt feelings, or misunderstandings. He could get to know her and then decide whether she could be the future Duchess of Holland or not.

Four

With a maid in tow, Sophie strolled the small park before Harlow and Lord Kemsley's London home. It was a little place of tranquility where she could watch London pass her by without interacting with too many people.

Certainly, the park had nannies and children running about, but parents were scarce, which suited her perfectly well. She walked along a garden with multiple roses planted, all in bloom and attracting the odd bee and ladybug.

She leaned down and smelled a yellow rose, the scent reminiscent of violets and lemon. Sophie looked about and, seeing a wooden bench, sat and opened her little notebook, writing down her findings before making a sketch of the plant she was explaining.

"You do take your hobby very seriously," a deep, masculine voice said at her side.

Sophie's stomach twisted in knots, as she recognized the voice from the evening before. She looked up, met the Duke of Holland's joyful face, and fumbled a reply she hoped did not make her look as discombobulated as she suspected.

"Your Grace, good afternoon." She closed her notebook and stood before dipping into a curtsy. "I enjoy my investigations, I suppose, and this afternoon there was no one at home, so I was free to come to the park," she explained. Was she rambling? Her flock of words certainly felt as though she was.

She sat and was surprised when he joined her, leaning back as if settling in for the day. "I live just around the corner from Kemsley. In fact, I think our back gardens have a linked hidden gate," he explained. "Although I have never found it."

"Really?" she asked, curious. "I may have to try to find it. I love mysterious tidbits like that," she said.

"Is that all the reason why?" he asked, pinning her with a stare that made the blood in her veins simmer. "I do not factor into your thoughts? If you find the gate, you can enter my gardens."

Heat bloomed on her cheeks, and for several moments she was not sure how to reply. Did he want her to be curious about him? Was he attempting to flirt with her in some way? "I did not mean my words to be misconstrued, Your Grace. I would never intrude if I were not invited to do so," she said, unsure if her explanation was any better than she had said before.

He smiled, and a little of her nerves dissipated. "I'm merely teasing, Miss York. But if you find the gate, do let me know. I often play cards and call on Kemsley, so not having to walk around an entire block would be most welcome."

"Walking is good for you," she stated. Certainly, taking in the duke's legs right now showed proof of that. Her gaze dipped to his thighs, casually spread on the bench in his tan, buckskin breeches. "Especially with the Season upon us and the opulent food we're fed at supper most nights. A little exercise ensures we fit out clothes comfortably."

"That is very true," he said, watching her momentarily. "May I read your little book of fragrance? Or do you not share it with anyone?" he asked her.

She handed it to him without hesitation. "You may read it if you like. There is nothing secret about it."

He ran his hand over the leather front before opening the book. He flicked through page after page of drawings and explanations before he stopped on one.

Wisteria ... "A purple, flowering vine that exudes a pungent scent that ranges from musky to a sweet aroma that can be strong to overpowering to some people."

He met her eye, his gaze dipping to her lips before moving back to the page. "I have Wisteria growing at Holland Hall. It is one of my favorite climbers, and I do not care how overpowering the scent is, I could sit and enjoy that fragrance all day."

Sophie could only imagine how beautiful his Wisteria and home would be. "How fortunate we are to have a similar interest. In London, it is not easy to find anyone who does not want to speak of horses or gambling or what ball or dinner is next and who will be there."

Sophie laid the book in her lap and rested her hands atop it. She looked at the rose garden ahead of them and thought over his words. "I do not know anyone, so worrying about who I shall see or what is planned has little interest for me."

"But your cousin, the countess, would like you to have a successful Season," he stated.

Sophie wasn't sure if it was a question or merely His Grace stating a fact. "Harlow would like me to marry, but I shall only do so with a man I can trust and love. If not, then I shall return home."

"And what will you do then?" he asked.

She frowned, debating if she ought to tell him or not. To do so was a risk, and he may stay well clear of her if she continued with the truth. But then, she could not abide liars in others and would not become one herself, not even before a duke.

"I shall have to find employment. A governess if I'm fortunate, or a lady's companion," she said, hoping she had not damned herself before him. She did not know him all that well, after all. For all she knew, he could run off to the *ton* and tell them of her common plans, and her Season would be over before it really began.

A GOVERNESS OR LADY'S COMPANION? Whatever Henry had expected Miss York to state, her reply was not it. Women who were governesses or lady's maids had fallen low and had no family to assist them, helping them out of the predicament they found themselves in.

Miss York was not that person. Her cousin was a countess, the other a viscountess. Surely she would not have to return home to find employment.

"But your cousins are Lady Kemsley and Viscountess Billington. Returning to Highclere will not be necessary, I'm sure," he stated, certain Miss York's family would never leave their cousin so poorly situated.

"I cannot expect her to support me, not when she is married with children. And I shall be perfectly fine working in such positions. As long as I'm safe, have a clean bed, and earn my wage honestly, I'm content."

Henry heard what she was saying, which was commendable, but also left him ill at ease. Why, he could not say, but she was so unassuming. Perhaps that was why he enjoyed speaking to her like they now were. If she were to go into service, they would never be able to talk so again.

He would never see her again, for that matter ...

But it was not his choice. She was not his family, and he could not persuade her to have a life the way he would like her to, no matter how much he wished to state that the thought of her working for her living seemed utterly unfair.

"Your Grace," a feminine voice said before him. Henry inwardly sighed before looking up at their uninvited guest. "Lady Leslie," he said, standing and bowing before the young woman, the sister to the Earl of Courtenay and one of the richest heiresses in London this year.

She smiled at him before casting a curious glance toward Miss York. "Enjoying the park, I see," Lady Leslie drawled, the smug, knowing look telling Henry that she was jumping to conclusions about him and Miss York that she should not.

Or perhaps she should ...

"I was on my way home from Whites and came upon Miss York enjoying the roses," he said, gesturing to the plants behind Lady Leslie." He paused. "Miss York, may I introduce you to Lady Leslie Courtenay? She is the sole sister to the Earl of Courtenay," he said.

Miss York stood and dipped into a curtsy, a wide smile on her lips that Lady Leslie did not replicate. "A pleasure," she said. "I did so admire your gown last evening, my lady. It was utterly spectacular."

Lady Leslie cast a dismissive glance toward Miss York that oozed dislike, if not distaste. "I do find talking of such subjects tedious," she drawled. "I always believe that when one speaks of fashion, they have little to talk about, and it is best to stop trying altogether."

Henry glanced at Miss York and noted her cheeks darkened to a deep red. He narrowed his eyes upon Lady Leslie, who seemed to register his displeasure.

"But I suppose," Lady Leslie stuttered, "it is a better subject to talk about than nothing at all. There is little worse than an awkward silence."

Henry cleared his throat, wishing to add there was nothing more disagreeable than a hoggish friend. "Well, we should not keep you, Lady Leslie. I was about to escort Miss York home before continuing on with my day. I wish you a good afternoon," he said, bowing and reaching for Miss York's hand before dragging her away from the waspish woman.

"Your Grace," Miss York chided him when they were several steps away from Lady Leslie. "You never afforded me the opportunity to wish her a good afternoon."

He scoffed, placing her hand atop his arm and holding it there. "Does it matter that you did not? I did not think she deserved one after her rudeness."

FIVE

S ophie had the urge to pinch her arm. She could not possibly be escorted home by the Duke of Holland and before the *ton*. She glanced around the park to see who else viewed this spectacular thing happening to her. An occasion that she would never forget and could not wait to tell Harlow about. How excited her cousin would be for her.

For a young woman from the country with little to offer, his escorting her was gracious indeed. To have a cousin who married well did not change her circumstances. Not in the way that mattered to gentlemen like Holland. He would marry a wealthy woman as high in the upper ten thousand as he was. Not a nobody like her.

But the duke did not seem to care about any of that. He walked toward Lord Kemsley's Georgian town house with his head held high and his easy conversation never stuttering into an awkward silence.

"Thank you for escorting me home, Your Grace. You are very kind," she said as they came before the front doors of her home.

"It was my pleasure. We're friends, are we not? And do not friends escort each other home at times?" His warm smile made the pit of her stomach flip, and she could not help but grin back at him.

With such delightful manners and charming words, a woman would be hard-pressed not to be swayed to swoon at such a man's feet. And the duke was very easy to admire and with sweet manners.

As much as she tried to deny herself, she watched him surreptitiously and couldn't remember when she had met such a rum duke. His kindness today before Lady Leslie proved that he was not flippant and cruel to cut her in front of others who were part of his social sphere.

"I'm glad to have you as a friend and that you escorted me home, Your Grace." Sophie bit her lip, not wanting their interaction to end. "Are you attending the Jenkins music recital this evening? I must admit that we do not have musical evenings in Highclere, so I'm loathe to miss it."

"I will be in attendance, yes. I'm fond of music, and I believe there will be an operatic singer."

"Yes," Sophie said, perhaps a little too lively than was necessary. She took a calming breath and fought not to tremble with the expectation of seeing him again. "A Maria Dickons. I have heard she's a talented singer and harpsichordist. A most entertaining night ahead of us."

He looked up at the door as she stepped onto the bottom step. The door opened, revealing Lord Kemsley's butler, watching them with interest. Sophie turned toward the duke. "Thank you again, Your Grace."

He lifted her hand and kissed the back of her gloved fingers. Sophie watched as his lips pressed against her glove. Her mouth dried, and she swallowed.

With a gulp.

"Until this evening, Miss York," he said, his eyes meeting hers but for a moment before he was off down the sidewalk, leaving her to gape after him like a besotted fool. She was starting to think she was well on the way to becoming so.

Before he could look back and catch her ogling him, she turned on her heel and entered the hall, only to find Harlow smirking at her from inside the door.

"Come into my parlor," Harlow said, waiting for her before they started toward the back of the house.

Sophie followed, pulling off her gloves as she went and untying her bonnet. The parlor was warm and smelled of roses, not to mention sunlight shimmered into the room by the floor-to-ceiling windows.

Harlow sat and patted the settee for Sophie to join her, settling her gloves, hat, and book at her side. The smirk she had noted before was now a pronounced smile of expectation. "Was that the Duke of Holland I saw escorting you home? What is this about? You must tell me everything," she demanded, wiggling on the chair as if she could not wait to hear what Sophie had to say.

Sophie thought back to the park and wondered how something so astounding could befall her. "We happened upon each other, that was all, and he was kind enough to escort me home." Sophie gathered her thoughts a moment, wanting to voice how she felt. "I must admit to feeling a little overwhelmed right now. I did not think a baron, nevertheless, a duke, would speak to me this year in London, nor wish to be acquaintances."

"And why would they not speak to you? You may not be an heiress, but you have far more superior assets than that. If a man marries you for your money, I believe there is not much hope for a successful marriage."

"That is true," Sophie noted the afternoon tea set out before them and took the opportunity to pour them both a fresh cup. She handed it to Harlow before picking up her own. "Please do not say a word to anyone, but I like the duke. My stomach twists and turns when I'm around him, and for some unknown reason, I've become obsessed with his lips," she admitted, needing to tell someone what was happening to her each time she saw the gentleman.

Harlow scoffed and coughed, placing down her cup with a clatter. "Oh, dearest, do not say such things when I'm taking a sip. I shall never keep my composure if you do." Harlow patted her arm. "So you desire him. Well, that is a good sign and a small step in perhaps many more."

Sophie shrugged but could not disagree. "When his lips touched the back of my hand earlier, I felt hot from head to toe. Have you seen the duke's lips? They're very ... very ..."

"Kissable?" Harlow interjected, smirking as if she knew something that Sophie did not. Which she had no doubt was the case since her friend was well and truly a married woman. A woman in love who sought her husband's touches and kisses.

"We have grown close, so would you tell me something if I asked?" Sophie hoped she would, but was not entirely certain.

"Of course," Harlow said without hesitation.

"Is kissing enjoyable with a man?" Sophie

asked. She did not want to remember the forced kiss Lord Carr bestowed upon her. Her lips had been bruised and swollen for a week, and not even cold compresses helped the pain he inflicted.

"Because we are the best of friends and cousins, I shall be honest with you. Kissing, my dearest Sophie, is one of the most sensual and enjoyable private things a woman and man can do. When Wes first kissed me ..." Harlow slumped against the back of the settee and sighed. "My toes curled in my silk slippers, and I thought I may perish of need. I'm certain that kissing Holland will bring about the same reaction I had with Kemsley. Certainly, if you feel like you do with the duke merely by being near him."

Sophie's stomach clenched at the thought. "While I do not think the duke sees me in such a way, it would be lovely to think he may in time. But we are friends, he said so himself, so at least I shall always have that."

"You may have more, do not discount yourself so early in the game. That Holland speaks to you is a favorable metier. It shows that he sees you as someone he can trust and converse with. Other marriages have started with less than that."

Sophie supposed that was true. "He's attending the Jenkins musical recital this evening. What gown would you suggest that I wear?" she asked. Her cousin was much more fashionable and knowledgeable of what gowns were best for the different events the London *ton* attended.

"The blue silk, this evening. We shall curl up your hair, and I'll lend you my diamond necklace, no other jewels, however. You shall look magnificent, and we shall see if the duke seeks you out again. If he does, it is with certainty that we can claim he likes you more than perhaps even he knows himself.

"Is that even possible?" Sophie asked, knowing little about how a man's mind worked or what they said could mean different things than what she thought.

"Of course, it is possible. Most gentlemen who court ladies give nothing away as to how they're feeling. At least, that is what I hear most often."

Sophie took in what Harlow said and tried to make sense of it all. The courtship game during the Season was more complicated than she first thought. But one thing she could do was look her best for anyone who may wish to converse with her.

"Would you mind if I bathe before this evening's recital? I want to look my best," she asked.

Harlow stood and pulled the bellpull next to the mantle. "I shall order you one now, so you may relax too. Nothing is too much for my dearest cousin. We shall have you married by the end of the Season and maybe even to a duke. How wondrous would that be?" she said, her smile wide.

Sophie enjoyed Harlow's enthusiasm while firmly keeping her feet on the ground. "Let us start with this evening musical, and we shall see how we go from there."

SIX

Sophie sat next to Harlow and Lord Kemsley for the musical recital held in Lord and Lady Jenkins Mayfair opulent home. Considering the night was a more intimate evening, no one would have guessed that to be the case since the Jenkins seemed to have invited enough acquaintances to produce a slight crush.

She closed her eyes and let the music wrap around her like a comforting embrace. The voice of Maria Dickons was powerful and cultured, captivating everyone in her presence. How clever the woman was and fortunate to have a voice like an angel and one people seemed to appreciate.

With everyone facing toward the singer, it made deducing who was present difficult, although Sophie believed she could make out the broad, muscular shoulders of the Duke of Holland. The gentleman turned to answer something from the lady at his side, and excitement thrummed through her that, indeed, he was here.

Her excitement was short-lived, however, when she realized it was Lady Leslie who was so fortunate as to sit beside him and keep him company. Did he like the young woman after all? At the park, she had assumed that not to be the case, but then maybe she was wrong. As for herself, she did not like Lady Leslie at all. Rude came to mind with the thought of her cutting tongue that would sever anyone in two should they get in her way.

They listened in awed silence for several songs before Maria Dickons required a short pause. The room dispersed for supper, and Sophie followed Harlow and Lord Kemsley toward the room where a light repast was laid out along with beverages.

"How lovely this evening is," Harlow said, handing Sophie a cup of tea with a small biscuit. "It makes a nice change from the hustle and overwhelming balls we're so often attending."

"I agree," Sophie said. They moved back into the music room, Lord Kemsley excusing himself to speak to the Duke of Derby.

"Holland seems engaged this evening with Lady Leslie," Harlow mentioned, glancing in His Grace's direction. "He ought not to show too much favoritism toward the young lady, or she will believe an offer is forthcoming. I heard Lady

Leslie's mama is determined for her daughter to marry well, and you cannot get any better than a rich, powerful duke."

Sophie nodded, unable to dispute that the duke in question, Holland, was indeed very well in looks, charm, and status. His Grace had everything a young lady would look for. His dark, mysterious eyes made one want to know secret things about him they should not.

As if he sensed their inspection of him, he glanced up from speaking to Lady Leslie. Their eyes met, held. Sophie would later tell herself that time stood still, that her heart ceased to beat in her chest. Indeed, her stomach fluttered like she was thrown into the air, just waiting to be caught.

He did not look away, and nor could she find the appropriateness to do so either. What was happening between them? Could she dream to hope? Or was she merely seeing possibilities where there were none? She had done so before. Her ability to trust people's characters was indeed flawed.

As if sensing the duke's attention elsewhere, Lady Leslie peeked over her shoulder and scowled at Sophie before turning back to Holland to continue their conversation. Whatever she said pulled his attention from her, and he averted his gaze, giving Lady Leslie his full engagement.

"You have a rival," Harlow said with a raised

brow. "And she does not seem to like that Holland has noticed you and likes what he sees."

"Do you think so?" Sophie stated, unsure of any of that. "I do not want my feelings injured by reaching too high. He is a duke, after all."

"And what is that? I was the same as you, and I married an earl. If whomever you marry loves you, their status does not matter."

Sophie debated her cousin's words of wisdom. "You may be right, but we're far from love." She glanced about the room and noticed the young maid standing beside a door in the parlor adjacent to the music room, directing ladies to the retiring room. "I shall return shortly. I need a moment before the second act begins." Sophie returned her teacup to a nearby footman and left the room. She finished her ablutions, only to return downstairs to find the door to the music recital closed and the muffled notes of singing behind the door.

She stood motionless, debating if it were appropriate to enter. How quickly had they started, after all? She had been gone barely five minutes.

"I see you've been shut out the same as I," a deep baritone said from behind.

Sophie spun about, having not expected to hear Holland at her back. "Your Grace," she said, dipping into a curtsy. "I have not been gone long, but it seems they were eager to begin again."

"So it appears," he drawled, holding out his

arm. "Shall we stroll the picture gallery? Lord and Lady Jenkins have quite a collection from artists many aspire to possess."

Without hesitation, Sophie linked her arm with His Grace's as they walked toward the picture gallery. "I should imagine you have just as grand a gallery as this one, possibly even grander," she said without thought.

Heat kissed her cheeks, and she glanced up at him, supposing he would find it abhorrent of her to speak of wealth. Instead, his lips twitched, and he shrugged in nonchalance. "You are right, it is a reasonable collection. Even my London home boasts a Rembrandt, but Holland Hall is the jewel in my collection, not just the picture gallery."

Sophie could well imagine. "It should be no surprise that I do not have such galleries. In fact, there are few portraits of myself in our home. Three if I'm counting correctly."

They came to a long, wide hall, paintings lining one side, sometimes two or three pictures high. "How beautiful this gallery is in the moon and candlelight."

Their eyes met, and again a hunger she had never encountered before thrummed through her. His attention dipped to her lips and to the diamond necklace Harlow had loaned her for the evening.

"I could not agree more at its unrivaled beauty," he said before pulling her along the Aubusson rug to inspect the paintings.

HENRY SHOULD NOT BE LEADING A young, unmarried miss down a darkened hall in the middle of a *tonnish* event, but nor could he deny himself. Running into Miss York was a pleasure after finally freeing himself from Lady Leslie.

Miss York walked alongside him, not the least overwhelmed by his presence, but more interested in the paintings on the wall. She pulled him to a stop before one featuring a vase of multiple varieties of flowers, a beautiful picture that caught his interest as well.

"What do you think this picture would smell like, should that be a possibility?" he asked, watching her pretty nose wrinkle in thought.

"Like spring," she said, grinning up at him. "Potent, rich florals from the hothouse, combined with the freshness of the wildflowers mixed within the bouquet."

Her smile hit him in the pit of his gut as hard as a prize fighter's fist. Her eyes glistened with delight, and he fought the overwhelming urge to kiss her. Never had he been possessed with such longing, but something about Miss York discombobulated his senses.

Without knowing what he was about, he

dipped his head and kissed those damn pretty lips that smiled with such sweetness that he ached.

He had to taste her, if only once.

Her small intake of breath hauled him to his senses, and he pulled back, but not before having felt how soft her lips were, like clouds of sin in heaven that beckoned him like nothing else ever had.

"I apologize, Miss York. I do not know what—"

He didn't finish his apology before her lips smothered his words. Henry, as sensually innocent as the woman in his arms, could not refuse her. Hunger, hot and indecent, tore through him, and he wrenched her into his arms, kissing her with a need that left him breathless, his head spinning, his body roaring for satisfaction.

He wanted her.

All of her.

In his bed.

The realization struck him, yet he could not stop tasting her, drawing her sweet tongue against his. Her hands slipped about his neck, her fingers twisting into the hair at his nape.

Thoughts of her on his bed. Her long, sun-kissed locks spilling over his pillows filled his mind. He wanted her, to make her scream his name in the throes of passion.

He lifted her off her feet, pressing her against him, and she moaned, the sound cracking what little restraint he possessed. He had never held a woman thus. He had never desired to do so, but something about Miss York made him lose all gentlemanly decorum and throw caution to the wind and take what he wanted instead.

"Holland," she gasped against his lips before he kissed her again. Their mouths fused, they clung to each together, seeking, needing to be touched. His cock rose to attention, and he clasped her bottom, undulating her against him, pursuing release in any way he could.

"Henry. My name is Henry," he managed to get out just as a door slammed somewhere deep in the house.

They stumbled apart, and Miss York glanced from one end of the room to the other. "I do not think anyone saw," he whispered, his words breathless.

She looked at him, her lips swollen and red, her eyes wide with both desire and fear. "I must go," she said, fleeing him without another word.

He ran a hand through his hair, let her go, swallowed hard, and fought for control.

A control he feared he would never gain back. Not now that Miss York was in town and his life, just where he wanted her.

SEVEN

S ophie returned to the music recital and slipped through the door, grateful that no one took heed of her when she sat at the back of the room where several chairs remained vacant.

Her lips tingled from the kiss she had just shared. One that she knew she wanted to do again, curse her wayward soul. How could she have allowed him to kiss her so passionately?

Because you are passionate about him, Sophie.

The music rose to a crescendo, and with the last notes from Maria Dickons, the room fell into applause as the music came to a delightful end. Sophie moved toward Harlow, needing her presence and support more than anyone right at this moment. Her mind jumped from thought to thought. Mocking her for the errors of her past to longing for a better future. Sophie did not know what to believe within herself or how to trust her judgment.

"Ah, there you are, Sophie. I lost sight of you when you excused yourself," Harlow said, linking their arms.

"There were quite a few ladies in the retiring room," she lied. "When I returned, the recital had already begun. I sat at the back of the hall, so as not to interrupt anyone's pleasure," she explained before Harlow started toward the door, Lord Kemsley on their heels.

"Tomorrow, we have the Craig's ball. An event not to be missed, so this evening concluding early will suit us, I think. We shall be well rested for tomorrow night."

Sophie nodded just as Holland entered the foyer from the direction of the picture gallery they had ambled through. His hair was askew as if he had run his hand through it several times, leaving him to appear even more handsome than he had before.

How could that be? But it was as true as her standing in the Jenkins's foyer. Or maybe she had run her hands through his dark locks. She tried to remember what had happened between them. The kiss so passionate, so consuming, and far too scorching for her to even now think straight. He had muddled her mind, and she could not calm the beating of her heart, no matter how much she tried.

She caught Holland's eye across the sea of heads, and hunger twisted in her belly. This was wrong. She could not seduce a duke. Could not give herself so easily to a man who would not offer any more than a dalliance.

Holland may say he was honorable, but past events told her men of his ilk were rarely so.

He may be, Sophie. Do not throw him aside so quickly.

She focused steadfastly on the door and the numerous carriages pulling up to the front of the house, hoping theirs soon would be one of them.

"Thank you for the evening, Harlow. It was my first time hearing such pretty music accompanied by an operatic singer. I will never forget it," Sophie said, knowing there was another reason she would not forget this night and the cause for that truth standing but feet away.

"Kemsley," she heard Holland call out, his deep voice making her want things she should not. They stopped and moved to the side of the walkway to allow others to leave. Sophie swallowed the nerves that threatened to choke her ability to breathe and watched with unhealthy fascination as Holland made his way over to them.

"I merely wanted to wish you a happy evening," the duke said, his gaze landing on her. Sophie was transported back into the picture gallery and fought not to give away her thoughts and the emotions that rioted within her. She schooled her features and offered a timid smile she had seen so many other ladies use in the past.

"Thank you," Kemsley said. "We're heading home, but I should think we shall see you at the Craig's ball tomorrow evening?"

"Of course," Holland said, nodding. "I would not miss it." His gaze flicked to her yet again, and Sophie looked to Harlow and found her friend, too, watching their interaction with interest.

"I hope you'll attend with the determination to dance, Your Grace," Harlow said, smiling at both the duke and Sophie.

Sophie inwardly cringed. Was her friend trying to matchmake them? The duke could make up his mind well enough without her friend's help, even if it were kindly meant. But she did not want to look desperate. Shame washed through her that she had allowed him to kiss her. Pull her against him in a shameful, fast way that no debutante ought to permit.

You kissed him back ...

Heat burned her cheeks, and she clamped her mouth shut.

"Of course," he replied. "And if Miss York is not otherwise engaged, perhaps she would do me the honor of granting me the first set?" Holland asked, picking up her hand and lifting it to his lips.

The moment his mouth touched the back of

her gloved hand, Sophie felt her mouth grow lax. Oh, dear. Oh, dear. This was too much. He was too sweet and handsome and everything she wanted but could not have. Not if she wanted to keep her feet firmly grounded in reality.

But oh, how could she not want to dance with him? Steal away to a darkened room and kiss him until her lips were numb and her body the opposite.

"I'm not engaged, Your Grace," she mumbled. "I will save the first set for you, of course," she heard herself reply, as if from another world.

She was not so uncertain that she was not floating away into space as it was, especially if the Duke of Holland kept looking at her as if she were the only thing that kept him on Earth.

HENRY SPENT THE REMAINDER OF THE night at Whites. The betting book lured his gaze several times before he stood and went to study the tome. A good many gentlemen's names had been added to the bet regarding Miss York, and he picked up the quill, wanting to remove his name from such antics.

"You know that's against the rules," Lord Bankes said, coming up to his side and picking the quill out of his hand.

Henry ground his teeth, not in the mood to

remain in a bet that he should never have signed up for to begin with. "The bet against Miss York isn't honorable, and I should never have put my name to it. Let me do what is right and remove the absurd stake entirely."

"Oh no, no, no," Lord Bankes said, slipping the quill into his coat pocket. "A bet is a bet, and as you're a gentleman, I would not think you'd go against your peers and act the coward. And in any case, you're doing better than anyone else regarding Miss York. You seem to be quite taken with the chit, more so than anyone else," Lord Bankes stated, much to Henry's shock.

Was that what people were saying about him.? Had they taken such an interest in the bet and those who had put their name to parchment that they were watching who was doing better than others? Who was courting the lady more than anyone else?

Henry frowned, not liking to be the latest on dit within the *ton*. "Miss York is friends with Lady Kemsley, and I'm friends with Lord Kemsley, as you well know. I'm not being overly friendly toward Miss York because of the bet. In fact, until this evening, I had forgotten that I had signed such a foolish bet," he lied.

"But we have not," Lord Bankes said with a smirk. "The young miss will not learn of it, so do not worry so."

"You're still here," the familiar sound of Lord Kemsley's voice said from behind Holland, and without thinking, he slammed the betting book closed and turned as if the devil himself were about to stab him in the back.

"Kemsley, I thought you were for home?" Holland said, stepping away from the book and placing his hand around Kemsley's shoulder, leading him to two empty wingback chairs and away from Lord Bankes, who could not be trusted not to say something about what he had put his name to.

"My darling wife and Miss York have ensconced themselves in Miss York's room, and they're going over the gown she is to wear tomorrow evening. I stated that I did not think it signified what either of them wore as they were lovely as they are, but my opinion was overridden," Kemsley said with a wry laugh.

His friend's words brought a grin to Holland's lips. He liked the image that came to mind of Miss York, excited for the night to come and what it could entail for her.

For you both, if you steal her away again ...

He would not. Tomorrow evening he would keep his head and not kiss her as he had this evening. But oh, what a kiss it had been. Of course, his reputation touted him to be a great lover, a rogue for all time, but he was not. No virgin could be. He rarely kissed indiscriminately and certainly not unmarried maids. But with Miss York, he could not have denied himself. Them both, if truth be told.

But he would tomorrow night. He had to.

Didn't he?

EIGHT

This evening Sophie felt like a princess. The empire-style gown was the most expensive, opulent dress she had ever worn. The dark-blue silk slid over her body, perfectly tailored to her height and dimensions, and accentuated all the womanly places men seemed to value.

Lord Bankes and his wandering gaze upon her bosom were no different. His delight at having her in his arms was evident, not to mention he had several times gushed how honored he was that she had bestowed upon him the first set.

The dance that she had reserved for the Duke of Holland, if he would ever bother to turn up and claim a dance with her.

Which he had not.

The country dance grew in tempo, and together they linked arms, spun, dipped between other couples, and laughed at the exuberance of the music.

What fun this evening had been so far, and it was only young. Her dance card was full, a bevy of gentlemen having all but swamped her the moment she arrived with Lord and Lady Kemsley. A delight if she were being honest with herself. After all, she was not the youngest of women in a sea of ladies newly out of the schoolroom, so to be asked to dance, offered supper and drinks, and have good conversation was pleasant.

"Have I mentioned, Miss York, how beautiful you are this evening? Like a rare sapphire that many gentlemen present would like to steal away."

Sophie raised her brow, unsure that his lordship's words were appropriate or worthy of a reply. She chose to ignore them and change the subject entirely.

"Lord and Lady Craig's ball is my fourth this Season, and yet each time I attend such an event, I'm struck by the beauty of the location and the people enjoying the night. I shall miss the glittering sights of London when I return home at the end of the Season."

"If you return home, Miss York. Perhaps you shall return newly married to your village," Lord Bankes said with conviction.

Heat kissed her cheeks, and she tried to remember what the etiquette was when a gentleman spoke of marriage to an unwed woman. From what she could recall, one ought to ignore such exchanges, but then, he was not wrong. Maybe she would fall in love and marry and never return to Highclere.

It would be best if she did not, considering who lived nearby …

"Thank you for being so confident in my Season, my lord, but I do not think we ought to discuss such matters as those of the heart."

He nodded and glanced yet again at her bosom. "You are right, of course. I've been remiss in my behavior, and we shall change the subject posthaste. What should we discuss, do you think? The latest on dit? I hear it is quite the scandal and involves a gentleman I do not believe you have met."

"Really?" she asked. "And pray tell who and what is this scandal you speak of?"

"Lord Carr is back from his extended honeymoon that lasted several years. It is rumored he only married the now Lady Carr, youngest daughter of Viscount Montfoot, because of her obscene dowry. All of London is speaking of it. I'm surprised you have not heard."

Lord Carr was in town?

Sophie's head swam, and she stumbled out of Lord Bankes' arms as memories she had repressed swamped her. Her stomach clamped into a hard knot, and she fought not to be ill.

"If you'll excuse me, my lord. A sudden headache," she lied, making her way to Harlow and the safety her cousin encompassed. Lord Carr was back in England? Was in London? No, it could not be true.

And like a scary novel she was reading late at night, the sight of his lordship himself, like a ghoul rising up from the dead to torture her yet again, appeared across the ballroom floor.

Sophie clasped her stomach and swallowed the bile that rose in her throat. The last time she had seen his visage, he had been atop her, grunting and groaning, telling her to be still, to stop fighting him, that she wanted it, had wanted him for so long that she needed to let him slake his need of her.

Sophie closed her eyes and took a deep breath. She could survive his presence. She had survived him once before. She could do so again.

"Miss York, my sincerest apologies for being late. I do hope I can claim at least one dance on your card this evening," the calming, deep baritone of the Duke of Holland said at her side.

Sophie met his gaze and hoped he could not see the distress that drummed through her like the instrument before battle. "My card is full, Your Grace. However, I do not think I shall dance again this evening. I'm not feeling my best," she said, hoping the vile churning of her stomach would stop. She did not want to cast up her accounts over the highly polished ballroom floor and ruin such a lovely ball for those in attendance.

No one knew her shame or what had happened, and she would do everything to keep it that way.

"You do appear pale. Would you care for some lemonade?" His Grace asked her, waving over a footman before taking two glasses and handing her one.

"Thank you," she said, forcing a smile on her lips and taking a welcome sip.

"Miss York?" Sophie's heart stopped beating, and without thought, she clasped the duke's arm for support before righting herself.

"Lord Carr, good evening," she said with the ability of the finest actress on the stage. No one would guess that the man she had known since childhood was the one man who sent terror through her blood. His mere presence, the very thought of having to speak and be polite, made her skin crawl. She wanted to maim him, have him cast out, and be shamed for his abhorrent behavior.

Not that anything of the kind would occur. Men were not shamed for their wrongs, only women. She would face the consequences of his lordship's actions and be the one cast out, ridiculed, and ruined.

"I was just informed you were in London," she managed, coolness to her words.

Lord Carr looked at the duke, and Sophie could see he was trying to garner what their connection could be and why the duke was standing so near, nevertheless speaking to her.

"How is it that you're in London, Miss York? I called on your mama, and she did not mention that I would see you here." His question made the pit of her stomach churn. Had he been to see her mama? Why would he do that? They had never been friends. And he was a husband now with a newly minted rich wife. What could he possibly wish to speak to her mama about?

"I'm in London visiting my cousin, Lady Kemsley," she said, wanting him to know that she wasn't without family or connections, even if he had always thought that to be the case. So much so that he had taken liberties that were not his to take.

"Your cousin is married to the Earl of Kemsley?" Lord Carr whistled and started to laugh, the tone one of disbelief and sarcasm.

She narrowed her eyes, fighting to keep her composure and not let his lordship's presence in town affect her. "Yes, my cousin. Harlow," she called, catching Harlow's attention, who walked over to them, taking her arm as if she sensed that Sophie needed her right now, which she did, very much so.

"Is everything well, my dear?" Harlow asked, looking to Lord Carr as if suspecting his presence disarmed Sophie.

"Lord Carr would like an introduction. Lord Carr, may I introduce you to my cousin, Lady Kemsley," Sophie said, feeling the duke's attention on her. What was Holland thinking? Did he wonder at her association with the viscount from her small village?

"A pleasure," Harlow said, but her tone did not convey warmth. Lord Carr, oblivious to what most women thought of him, did not pick up on the cue that his presence was not entirely welcome.

"The pleasure is all mine," Lord Carr said. "I've had a lovely little tête-à-tête with your cousin. May I be permitted to call? We have so much to recount. Always a pleasure to see Miss York."

"Hmm, yes, I can see why you would think that, but I'm afraid we're quite busy with our entertainments, which means little time to host anything at home. But I'm sure we shall see you at certain balls and parties, such as this evening."

Relief swamped Sophie that Harlow had sensed her dislike of Lord Carr and had put paid to his attempt to see her outside such events where they were not present. She did not want to see him. He could burn in hell for all she cared.

If only he would leave so she could speak to

the duke. The vexing man had too much nerve to remain with them as if he were wanted around them.

"I believe Lady Carr is gesturing to you," Sophie lied, nodding in the direction of his wife, who was in deep conversation with several women and not the least caring as to where her husband was.

Lord Carr glanced in his wife's direction. He turned back to them, his eyes narrowing on Sophie but a moment before he laughed, all jovial once again.

She glared, no longer the fifteen-year-old girl with so little that he thought he could take everything from her without retribution. They were not friends, nor were they ever, and the sooner Lord Carr learned that truth, the better, even if she had to tell him to his face.

NINE

The notes of a waltz sounded, and Henry held out his hand for Miss York to take, not willing to miss his chance at having her in his arms once more. "Please dance with me," he asked, not so high in the instep not to beg.

Thankfully, Miss York took his hand without hesitation, and he led them onto the dance floor.

He settled her in his arms, a feeling of contentment coming over him at her being so near once more. "I did not know Lord Carr was from Highclere. I should imagine having a friend from your village here in town would be quite a comfort. A little piece of home in London."

Miss York's gaze widened before her visage crumbled into something that resembled revulsion.

"No matter what Lord Carr implies, we're not friends, Your Grace. He did not circulate in the same social spheres I did back home. I was his grandmother's companion, nothing more."

Henry frowned, unsure if that was true, but neither did he want to spend his entire evening speaking about another man. Nor did Miss York seem inclined to say much about his lordship and their entwined past.

He cleared his throat, needing to discuss other matters that had plagued him since last evening. "About our stroll in the picture gallery, Miss York," he began, needing to explain his actions and try to make amends for them. What he had done were not the actions of a gentleman. Miss York deserved the opportunity to scold him for his wayward urges.

Urges that even now, he found challenging to school.

"You have nothing to apologize for, Your Grace. You were not the only individual taking part in that kiss." The memory of her lips sent a bolt of desire to his groin, and he could not help but ponder what had happened to the sensible, clear-thinking duke he had always been up until meeting her.

His virginity at this very moment seemed like a noose around his neck. Had he not been so, he could enjoy other nightly pursuits with women of looser morals and slake the burning, aching need whenever he was around Miss York.

Worse was the realization that now he knew

Miss York, the thought of rutting some unknown woman and paying a fee felt soiled and unsatisfying.

He met Miss York's clear, blue eyes and lost himself in their depths. No, he could not rut with just anyone. Not when his sole desire was the woman in his arms.

The fervor was unlike anything he had ever known, raw and unfamiliar. A fact about himself he did not know how to control or soothe.

His lips twitched at her answer, and without thinking, he pulled her closer, the hem of her dress covering his highly polished boots and parts of his knee-high silk breeches. "As pleasant as the interlude was, we cannot participate in such activities again. You're a maid, and I'm a duke, and we're both unmarried. We court scandal if we're come upon."

She tipped up her head, and he marveled at how beautiful and unassuming she was of that fact. He knew she saw herself beneath him, which may be true socially, but her inner beauty was just as great as his and her passion too. Those were amendable qualities he liked far more than rank. He was a duke, after all. Who was to tell him who he could and could not court?

Do not forget your bet.

The reminder made him inwardly wince, and he cursed himself a fool for adding his name to the betting book. One he had never taken part in before. What had he been thinking? He supposed he wanted to be part of the club. One of the boys. The rogue everyone thought him to be.

"I did not think scandal scared you, Your Grace. In fact, before the Season commenced, I read that you were come upon in a compromising position with a certain famous opera singer. At least the paper alluded to the fact that it was you."

A cold chill ran down his spine, and he took a misstep, tripping before righting himself. "Apologies, Miss York." He cleared his throat, heat kissing his cheeks. Was there such an article? If so, he had missed that particular untruth. "I do not know anything of the kind, Miss York. And as for the matter you read, I can guarantee I was not caught with anyone."

Miss York raised her brow, clearly doubting his words. "Was she a titled widow then, or a singer? Shall we see her on stage during one of the nights at the theater?" Miss York further questioned.

He let out an annoyed breath. Was she not listening to him? "I have not acted such a cad. I promise you," he said, hoping she would believe him.

She tipped her head to the side, studying him, and he could see she was trying to deduce if he was stating the truth. "Very well, I shall not question you further on the article, and I must admit that I'm glad there is no validity to it."

Henry wondered if she had meant to be so frank with her words. A dark, rosy hue blossomed on her cheeks, and he knew she had not. "So you do not like the idea of me courting other ladies? How very interesting, Miss York."

And very revealing.

Sophie fought to school her features and to cull her wayward tongue that wanted to spill her innermost thoughts to the man in her arms. But he was so charming. There was an innocence about him that called her to be honest. To tell him that the idea of him with anyone other than herself left a sour taste in her mouth.

"Let me ask you this, Your Grace. Do you like the idea of me being courted by another gentleman?" There, she had been bold and brave and asked what had been burning in her mind since their wicked kiss. A kiss that she wanted to experience again.

Although she could not say why, she trusted the duke. There was no secretive vague speech that left her wondering if he were sincere or not. Unlike other people in her past, he did not seem to have a disingenuous bone in his body.

His eyes narrowed at her question before he

said, "The idea makes my blood run cold." He dazed her with his honest response.

Her stomach twisted in knots, and she leaned close, breathing deep the scent of sandalwood and man. An intoxicating combination that left her mind spinning at the thought of them.

"This is madness," she admitted. "We should not be speaking to one another in such a way."

"And yet, I cannot help myself. I will not shy away from what I desire. Say pretty things that may or may not mean something. I like you more than I thought I would like anyone this Season, and you ought to know my truth."

His words were as sweet as the ices from Gunter's. "I'm not deserving of you, Your Grace," she said, the knowledge of her past urging her to be cautious. If he found out the truth of her time at Highclere, he would shun her, no matter how close they became in the interim, and she could not bear that. "I know I'm not acceptable to you or your family, and we should end this madness before we take it too far."

He shook his head, the line between his eyes severe. "You have not lied, and I know you have no dowry, and nor do I care. Whomever I choose to be my wife and duchess, I hope that I choose because I come to care for her, love her above anything else in the world."

Sophie nodded, hoping that would be the case for her too. "If we're to spend more time together, and I know the Season is young, we must be discreet and not give in to urges that could force our hand. I do not want you to regret your choice, whatever it may be. But I would like to spend more time with you. Learn more about you and your life and see if we're a good match."

His fingers slipped about her waist, sending a delicious shiver up her spine. "I think that is a tenable idea and one I would like to start posthaste. I want to know all about you, your life before London, your hobbies and dislikes."

Sophie marveled at him, having never considered meeting a gentleman like the duke. How could he be so caring? The rumored rogue who had a different lover each week. This was not the man in her arms who wanted to know Miss Sophie York's humble life so he could decide whether to merge it with his. But even with all that stood between them, she wanted to try.

"Shall we start with your favorite animal, Your Grace?" she asked. "I'm excessively fond of cats and have a blue-eyed doll at home. She is so affectionate and allows me to carry her around whenever I please."

Just at that moment, the dance came to a reluctant end. The duke led her off the floor to the side of the room. "I like horses particularly, but I, too, have a house pet. A wolfhound called Apollo. I've never had a cat before."

"I've never owned a dog before," she admitted. "Does that mean we're too opposite in taste to achieve what we hope to?" she asked him, her heart halting its beat while he thought about her question.

"I think it makes us perfectly matched. How boring would our life be if we only enjoyed the same things?"

Sophie smiled, supposing that to be true. "I had not looked at it that way." But now that he mentioned it, the idea held more merit than she first gave it credit.

TEN

The following evening Sophie settled in the Kemsley box at The Theatre Royal on Drury Lane. She sat behind Harlow and Lord Kemsley, unable to stop the expectation that this evening she would enjoy a small production of *Henry V*.

The second level of the theatre was full to the brim with the *ton*. Lords and ladies, most of whom she had been introduced to over the last several weeks, settled into their seats and prepared themselves for the night's entertainment.

Sophie took in the crowd, wondering if Holland was present. Did his family have one of the stylish boxes which sat separately from the others and were more opulent? She had forgotten to ask him if he were to attend, but indeed with everyone else here this evening, so too would he be, she would imagine.

She caught sight of Lord Carr, seated beside

his wife on the first level and where others who did not own boxes sat. His eyes narrowed back at her, and she wondered what he was thinking. His minute nod in acknowledgment was his only action to let her know he had noticed her.

Sophie tipped up her nose and turned her attention to the stage as the orchestra prepared their instruments for the evening. How she wished he had not come to town. Why could he not have stayed in Highclere until she married and moved away, so she would never have to see his awful, fiendish face again?

The curtain to their box opened, and Sophie turned to see Holland enter. She bit her lip, stifling a sigh at seeing him, tall and handsome in his superfine coat and highly starched and perfectly tied silver cravat.

"Apologies, Kemsley, Lady Kemsley, Miss York," he said, bowing. "I was caught in the foyer by Lord Bankes, and he's difficult to remove oneself from."

Kemsley laughed, and Sophie smiled, pleased he was here after all and looking to stay with them through the evening.

"No trouble at all, Your Grace," Harlow said, her eyes meeting Sophie's but a moment. "We're glad you could join us. We'll make a merry party indeed."

"Undoubtedly," Holland said, his voice low with meaning. He met Sophie's eyes, and she inwardly sighed. How was she to conduct herself suitably around such a perfectly delightful man? He was everything she had dreamed of in a husband. It seemed almost unbelievable that he was here and interested in her. A nobody, penniless woman from Highclere.

His lips twitched as if he knew what she was thinking, and yet again, she was reminded of how soft they were when she kissed him. Damn her wayward soul, but she wanted to kiss him again.

What happened to being cautious, Sophie? Remember what happened the last time you placed trust in a gentleman?

Sophie pushed the wretched thought aside. Her mistake happened years ago. No longer would she take responsibility for what happened to her. She had pleaded with Lord Carr to stop and had not desired what he forced on her.

The memory sent a cold shiver down her spine, and she clutched her hands together in her lap as a wave of nausea washed over her. She breathed deep, fought to forget, to move past, and forgive herself for the hundredth time.

Holland's hand slipped into hers and squeezed tight. She met his eyes and saw nothing but concern. "I do not know what bothers you, but I hope it is not I?" he whispered.

Her heart ached at the thought of him thinking such a thing. Nothing could be further from the truth.

She closed her fingers around his. "A slight chill in the air, that is all," she lied. The secret she carried and the shame she hoped would one day leave her had not in the years since that dreadful night. Until Lord Carr's arrival in London, she had not seen him, but having him speak to her and watch her as he had been earlier left her feeling as vulnerable as she had been that awful night he came after her.

Holland's thumb rubbed soothingly over the top of her hand, and she closed her eyes, reveling in his touch. The duke was a kind man, a gentleman who had been honest with his intentions. If they continued to grow close, there was a possibility that she would be a duchess before the end of the Season.

The idea seemed impossible, but how she would love to fall in love. Be loved by the man at her side.

"You're magnificent this evening, Miss York," he whispered, the breath of his words kissing the whorl of her ear.

Sophie turned and met his eyes. They were so close, but a whisper between them and an overwhelming urge to close the space that separated them teased her self-control.

His eyes dipped to her lips, and she knew he was thinking the same. Her heart skipped a beat, and his hand tightened on hers. A muscle worked on his jaw before he blinked and drew back. "You tempt me more than I care to admit to," he whispered for only her to hear.

Did she? Sophie had never heard such sweet words uttered to her before. Was it all a ploy? One part of her mind railed at the duke's comments while the other side reveled in them. Surely being friends with Kemsley, he was trustworthy. She had never known her cousin or the earl to be bad judges of character.

"Are you in earnest?" she asked him, unable to believe she could tempt a duke. She was nobody, a country mouse with no dowry and very little to recommend her.

He frowned at her question as the actors commenced Act I of the play. "You should not discredit yourself so easily, Miss York. I would not say what I had unless I were speaking the truth. You know I want to see more of you."

Heat mixed with need thrummed through her at his words, and she shuffled closer to his side. "When can we see each other again?"

"May I call on you tomorrow for afternoon tea? Perhaps we can picnic in Kemsley's outside pavilion overlooking their small pond."

The idea was too extraordinary to decline. A few moments alone with Holland was perfection. "I shall ask and have a note sent over in the morning letting you know if you're permitted." Sophie paused, biting her lip and hoping her next words were not too forward. "Please call me Sophie when we're alone. Will you do that for me?" she asked him.

He flipped her hand and laid it against her leg, running his finger across her palm, sending a frisson of sensation down her spine. Never had she ever experienced something so compelling. Her body did not feel like itself. Her heart beat fast, and heat prickled her skin.

"Only if you agree to call me Henry, I shall do the same for you," he said, a small smile playing about his lips.

Henry ... "I would like to call you Henry," she said.

The hunger that burned in his dark-brown eyes told her there was more between them than she dared ever dream. The duke was courting her. How had such an amazing turn of events happened?

He adjusted his seat, taking her hand and placing it out of sight between them. His fingers entwined with hers, and she was lost. The play filled the room with drama and encased them all in the magic of the night. A night she would never forget.

"I did not know you would be joining us this evening," she whispered, leaning close to his side. "I'm glad that you're here."

"I ran into Kemsley at Whites and asked if he would permit me to attend with you. I would have traveled with you all from Mayfair, but I was waylaid."

"Well, I'm glad you're here now," she admitted. Was she too forward telling him her regard? Possibly, but nor did she see the point of remaining coy and secretive. How was he to know she returned his feelings if she did not show him? He was an honorable man, and she could not paint every gentleman she ever met with the same brush as Lord Carr.

He met her eye and held her gaze, not the least in a rush to return his attention to the play on the stage. "I have wanted to spend more time with you, as you well know. On such nights, we can at least sit near each other and converse. Balls and parties are all very well, but dancing is merely several minutes, and then we're to part again. I have you all to myself this evening, and if we whisper, we can continue our conversation all night."

Sophie chuckled, schooling her features when Lady Smithfield in the box next to theirs scowled in their direction. The duke waggled his brows at her ladyship, and she flipped out her fan in disgust, chastising them with her sharp movements, if not words.

"I think you have displeased her ladyship," Sophie stated, turning away from the woman.

"Her displeasure is worth it if it means I'm with you," he said, dipping his head. "And if we were anywhere but here, I would kiss you, Sophie."

Sophie understood his need, such as it was so much like hers. "I would like that too. What a shame we cannot."

He shrugged. "The night is young yet. Do not discredit me so easily."

She would not.

Eleven

I ntermission could not come soon enough for Henry, and excusing himself, he left the box. A glass of whisky was what he needed. Something, anything to try to quell the burning desire he had for Sophie sitting beside him. A temptation that he could not taste. Not in the box, in any case.

He closed his eyes, taking a calming breath, and could still smell the lingering scent of strawberries that hung about her, making her smell good enough to eat.

What had happened to him these past days? He was not himself, and the more time he spent with Sophie, the more he wanted her in all the delicious, debase, sexually arousing ways a man could have a woman.

Not that he knew much of what that entailed, but damn, he would like to learn with her.

A prickling of concern thrummed through him with each stride down the hall that he would not be enough for her. His lack of experience and inability to really know what he was doing would disappoint her.

Surely that would not be the case. She was a maid, after all. How much could she know of what happened between a man and woman when they were intimate?

He had nothing to be ashamed of but did not want to leave her unsatisfied. As much as he had read extensively on what occurred during the sexual act, everything seemed foreign and odd to put into practice.

He came to the top of the stairs leading down to the foyer and spied several footmen with trays of refreshments. He went downstairs and took a glass of champagne, downing it just as other guests started to swamp the foyer.

Finishing his drink, he returned upstairs and found several other guests in the box he shared this evening, but Sophie was not one of them. Stepping out into the corridor, determined to find her, he spied her going into the lady's retiring room several doors down.

He could not meet her there. That would not do at all. They had agreed to be discreet while they got to know each other. Forced to marry now may lead to a mistake they would both regret, and he could not stomach that. She deserved only the best.

He strolled down the hall, pacing as close to the retiring room as he could without appearing too strange. Several ladies leaving the room threw him odd looks, but he merely smiled, confusing them further. Sophie stepped out into the corridor and caught sight of him, a small smile playing about her lips.

"You disappeared with haste," she said, a little circumspection to her tone he wished he had not placed there.

He walked them along the corridor before stopping at an empty box. Taking her hand, he slipped them into the darkened space, the angle of the box shielding them from view of everyone there.

"I was parched," he admitted, moving toward her. "I needed a drink."

She stepped backward until the wall stopped her progress. "What are you doing, Your Grace?" she asked him, a slight quake to her words.

He took in her beauty. A true diamond unaware of her worth. The urge to taste sensual lips wrapped about his need and tugged hard. He wanted her to touch him, kiss him, soothe the ache he knew they both must feel.

You're in the theater! Stop being cockish!

"I'm parched too." Sophie slipped her hands

around his neck, and he lost all sensible thought. He did not want to be an upstanding, virginal duke. Not when it came to the woman in his arms. He wanted her to want him as much as he craved her, and from the burning hunger in her eyes, he understood she did.

Henry clasped her jaw, tipped up her pretty face, and claimed her lips. He moaned at the satisfaction that purred through his soul at being with her like this again. All thoughts of being soft and beguiling vanished in an instant. He kissed her hard, deep. Their tongues tangled, danced, and drew him toward need like nothing else ever had.

She did not shy away from his kiss. She threw herself into their game of seduction. His body hardened, and he closed the space between them.

Her body against his, her breasts pressing against his chest, their ragged breaths mingled. Henry clasped her hip, teasing his cock with her body. She gasped through their embrace and did not run from what she did to him. Instead, she moaned, clung to him, and bedeviled him to a fever pitch.

His balls hardened. His cock straining for discharge against his breeches. He broke the kiss and reached for the hem of her dress, lifting it up so he could touch her. He needed to feel her body, tease and give her pleasure.

When his hand stroked over her sex, she murmured his name like a Siren's song and did not thwart his ministrations. She set her leg against his hip, presenting more opportunities to touch her.

He kissed her neck and licked his way along the softness of her skin as his hand played with her body like a musical instrument. She was wet, satiny, and pliant in his arms. He stroked her, found what she enjoyed most, and did not relent.

He wanted to hear her scream his name. He wanted to see her come apart in his arms, just as the books described.

"Henry." She clasped his jaw and kissed him, deep and long. He lost himself in their kiss, reveled in the taste of her.

He slipped a finger into her aching core, mimicking what intercourse would be like, and realized that he had missed out on so much being the upstanding duke he had always been.

To have a willing woman, a woman who wanted the touch of a man as much as he desired to touch her, was an elixir he could no longer deny himself.

"Do you like it?" he asked, flicking his thumb over her nubbin.

She nodded, her heavy-lidded eyes meeting his momentarily before she closed them again. "I do not know what you're doing, but it feels utterly wonderful."

Her words were nothing like he'd heard before, but blast it all to hell, they were enticing.

He could not miss this moment and watched, entranced as pleasure crossed her features. As her body rode his hand, her fingers clawing into his shoulders as she came in his arms.

The image was too much, and he felt his balls tighten before he spent in his breeches like a green virginal lad experiencing sex for the first time. He supposed that was not untrue.

After several moments her gaze met his, and he could see the wonder in her blue eyes. A surprise that he, too, felt.

They were different together. Something told him they ought to be together, not just this night but all nights to come.

"I feel as though I should say thank you." A pretty blush stole across her cheeks. They disentangled themselves and put a modest space between them.

He shook his head, unable to voice all that he was thinking right at this moment. "You do not owe me anything. But I will call on you tomorrow, but for now, I must leave."

"You're leaving?" she exclaimed, reaching for him so he could not go.

"I have to leave, Sophie. The events of this evening mean that I've not come away from our little interlude unscathed."

She frowned, stepping back and looking him up and down. "You appear perfectly fine to me. What do you mean?" she asked.

He clasped her cheek and stole another kiss. "I spent in my breeches if you must know. Watching you find pleasure was too much for me, and I need to return home and bathe."

"Really?" Her tone dripped with seduction and interest. "So if I were to touch you here, I would know you do not state a lie?"

She did as she teased, and he sucked in a startled gasp. Her palm stroked him, and he closed his eyes, his cock hardening again at her touch.

"You would have me leave with a hard cock pressing against my breeches as well as a wet patch?" he asked, unable to bite back his grin.

She smiled, not the least interested in stopping her administration against his person. "I wish you had told me you were as affected as I was by what we were doing. I would have touched you too. Made it more enjoyable."

"Oh, it was satisfying, Sophie." He pulled her into his arms and held her close. "I shall call on you tomorrow, and we shall have another satisfying time together. And if I should hold a trump hand, we shall have a moment or two alone, so I may watch you shatter in my arms yet again. This time I'd like to hear my name on your lips."

"There would be no other name I would utter." She placed little kisses against his jaw, along his neck before, unable to wait a moment longer, he took her lips in a searing kiss.

Tomorrow could not come soon enough. Not for either of them.

TWELVE

Sophie sat at the breakfast table alone with Harlow and tried not to draw attention to herself, which was not an easy accomplishment after her escapades with Holland the night before.

The memory of his touch sent a thrill of delight and longing through her. She wanted him to touch, kiss, and whisper wicked, naughty things in her ear.

His reaction to their desire last evening was almost as naïve as hers in a lot of ways. A realization that went against everything that she knew of the duke. He was Holland: a rakehell, a man who, over the years, had many lovers. The papers said it was so, not to mention gossip. But the image did not make sense to her. Not after he found release without her even touching his person.

Did he genuinely desire her so much that such a thing could happen to a man?

"The duke asked Kemsley last evening to picnic with you today on the grounds. Is this what you would like to do?" Harlow asked, dabbing her lips with her napkin before laying it on the table.

A footman cleared away the countess's breakfast before pouring her a fresh cup of tea.

Sophie cleared her throat, choosing her words wisely. If she appeared too keen, Harlow would sense something had changed between them and could be cautious. "I would like to have a picnic with His Grace. He's been attentive, and I get along well with the duke. If you think it would be suitable, I would like to spend more time with him, away from the gossiping *ton* and prying eyes."

Harlow leaned back in her chair and studied her a moment. "I do not mind Holland picnicking with you. It is a way for you both to court and decide if you're a match." She paused. "Kemsley is away this afternoon, so he will not intrude on your luncheon with the duke with idle chatter about horses or politics, so the timing is perfect in that regard. But what about a chaperone? Do you wish for me to sit outside with you both, or would you prefer a maid?"

Sophie wondered how she would say what she was about to. "Do you think it would be at all possible for us not to have a chaperone? Surely having a picnic in the gardens is not so very scandalous. No one will see us and know that we're somewhat alone on the grounds other than yourself. I think it would be difficult to be as honest as we would be should someone be hovering nearby, especially a servant." Sophie crossed her fingers under the table and hoped that her cousin, who had not been so innocent herself when Kemsley courted her, would see the logic in her words.

"Hmm," Harlow hedged. "The duke is renowned for being a buck. I'm not certain that it is safe for you to be alone with him."

Sophie shook her head. The duke was no less innocent than she was herself, even if that were not a decision she had chosen for herself. But, like it or not, she was no longer a maid and did not need a chaperone for something she could not lose again.

"Harlow, I love you dearly, as well you know, but I also know you were not so discreet when Kemsley was courting you. Please give me this afternoon with the duke. I shall not cause a scandal, and we will be but talking in the pavilion. Nothing will happen," she stated, hoping that were true.

She would try to behave herself and not fall under his charms that he had so very many of. A kiss or two would not hurt anyone, especially the *ton* if they did not ever find out about it.

"I should not allow it. Your mama would scold me should she discover I permitted such a visit, but I do see your point and will allow your request this time. I suppose it is no different should he have taken you on a carriage ride into the country."

Sophie smiled, unable to hide her relief at having this time with the duke to herself. "Thank you, Harlow. You are too wonderful for words. I promise we shall eat, talk, and not much else."

Harlow raised her brow at her words. "I know it is often difficult with these great handsome men not to give way to passions, but I do not want to see you get hurt, Sophie. That is my only concern. He has not offered his hand, and therefore there is a chance he will not. Do not give him all of yourself without being certain he is the man for you. The man you want to marry and spend the rest of your life with."

Sophie took in Harlow's words. All valid points and many she had thought herself these past days together. But there was something about the duke that was different. He was honest, and she was confident he would not lead her amiss. And if he did, he would do right by her.

"I will not do anything I'm uncomfortable with, Harlow. I promise you."

THE DUKE ARRIVED AT PRECISELY ONE o'clock in the afternoon. Sophie met him in the foyer, and after greeting Harlow, she escorted him out of the house through the back parlor doors and toward the pavilion where they would break their fast.

As agreed, no servant followed them out onto the lawns, and for several minutes they strolled the Kemsley gardens, taking in the large trees and breathing deep the sweet perfumes the gardens afforded them at this time of year. The pretty pavilion and its privacy in the distance lured them with every step.

"I see we're all set for our picnic," the duke said, slipping his fingers about hers and holding her hand as they viewed the table setting Sophie had overlooked earlier.

The innocence and sweetness of his gesture made hope well within her. He was so sweet that even now, he tempted her to tilt her head up toward his and let him kiss her senselessly.

"I hope you like what I've done. I've overseen it myself," she admitted.

They slowly made their way closer. The pavilion was a circular building, but only the front was open to the elements, giving a view of the pond and gardens.

A daybed, a small, circular table that could seat four persons, and a small fireplace encompassed the room. Their lunch sat under silver dish covers, keeping their fare warm. A bottle of champagne sat chilling in an ice bucket beside the table.

Sophie marveled at the pretty picture the picnic made and would ensure she thanked Harlow for allowing her to enjoy her time with the duke when she saw her next.

"Shall we sit? It looks wonderful," Like the gentleman Henry was, he pulled out her chair and helped her to sit, his eyes never leaving hers as he went around the table and found his seat.

Heat kissed her cheeks at the determination and hunger that burned in his brown eyes. She fought to still her beating heart lest he hear what he did to her. "Shall we have a drink?" Sophie reached for the bottle, nerves getting the better of her.

He waved her hand aside, picking up the bottle himself. "Allow me." He poured them both a glass in the crystal goblets, and Sophie took a fortifying sip. Why she felt shy and out of sorts made little sense. They were friends, had kissed, and more than that. There was no reason why she should be so discombobulated.

Unless you care for him and his affection far more than you thought ...

All true, she supposed. She did care for him and his opinions. One reason why he could never find out what had happened to her in Highclere. He would think poorly of her, think her a slattern out to fool him. The thought dulled a little of her excitement for the afternoon.

"I see we're quite alone today." Holland glanced out into the gardens, a small, playful smile on his lips. "Is this by design, or are we just fortunate that it is so?"

"I asked Harlow for us to be unchaperoned. Considering we're in the gardens, I did not consider that scandalous. She agreed after a healthy debate, so long as we act respectably."

He pursed his lips, sipping his wine. The cheeky smile he bestowed afterward sent butterflies through her belly. "I cannot stop thinking about you, Sophie. You must know that I'm not courting anyone else, and only you populate my every thought."

"In truth?" she replied. "You are all that occupies my thoughts, too."

He stood and came to kneel beside her chair. He clasped her hips, moving her so they could come face-to-face. "Last night at the theater. I should not have taken such liberties. You're innocent, a debutante, and I acted in an ungentleman-like manner."

She closed her eyes, wishing she were innocent, as he stated. She supposed, in some ways, it was true. She had never had such passion, care, and sweetness before in her life. Her past was haunted by nothing but pain and fear.

But with Henry, their interactions were so different.

"I'm not so naïve. I do not wish to be innocent with you," she admitted, trying to be as truthful as possible.

"I'll be the judge of that," he said before she lost herself in his kiss.

THIRTEEN

He should stop. They were in the garden where they could be come upon by anyone at any moment, and yet, all Henry could think about, all he had dreamed about, was Sophie.

Having her in his arms once again. Kissing her delectable mouth, the feel of her in his arms pressing against him was an elixir he could no longer live without.

He would not apologize or shy away from how she made him feel. If he were being frank with himself, she made him feel things he never had before—virile, a man, a lover, and a friend.

Would she believe your feelings should she learn of the bet?

He cast the negative thought aside. He was not kissing Sophie now, spending time with her because of the stupid bet he had put his name to. Had he met her before laying quill to parchment, he would still be where he was right at this moment. He knew that truth to his very core. And what did the bet matter now? Sophie would never come to learn of it. There were hundreds of bets placed every year, and many ladies were the source of those wagers, just like the others in the past. Sophie, too, would never have to concern herself with knowing what he had done.

It meant nothing in any case. He was here for her, and no stake would have ever changed that.

She clung to him as he did her. Two souls unwilling to part no matter the danger. But they could not remain so. It was too risky here. Too many servants, gardeners, Lord or Lady Kemsley who could come upon them.

Henry drew back, tipping up Sophie's face to meet her eyes. "It seems that I'm not myself whenever I'm around you."

She grinned, and he marveled at her beauty and sweetness. "Who are you normally then?" she asked teasingly.

He stood and taking her hand, drew her toward the small, round table with their picnic set out before them. "A man who does not kiss young, unmarried ladies in pavilions in their cousin's garden." He held out her chair, and she sat, thanking him.

"That's not what I've heard, Your Grace."

"Henry, please," he reminded her. "And you should not always believe what you hear about a person, especially when it comes to the gossip that floats about the *ton*. It's often incorrect."

"So you're not the rogue you're painted to be? Your kisses would say otherwise."

Shame washed through him that she thought that of him. Thought that he was only here because it was his second nature to seduce women. How far from the truth that was. "I'm no rogue, and I certainly do not seduce unmarried ladies in gardens whenever the opportunity arises. You, my darling Sophie, are an exception to my rule."

He reached across the table, took her hand, and played with her fingers. They were free of gloves and long, her nails tidy and narrow, simply perfect in his opinion. "Tell me more about yourself. I want to know everything there is about your life and family. You have a mother. Will she be coming to London this Season?"

Sophie linked her fingers with his and leaned across the table. "I'm only child and did not have many friends growing up. We are by no means affluent, Henry. You should understand that I do not falsify that truth. I bring nothing to a union, nothing of monetary value at least."

"You bring yourself, and that is enough for me. I do not need or want anything more." He hated that she thought he and so many of his ilk needed to marry an heiress, a titled lord's daughter with connections. He did not care about any of those things so long as he had a wife who was honest and kind and, without any fortune at all, had affection toward her husband.

Him ...

"You're very sweet to say so, but you are the exception, not the rule here in London. But, the town of Highclere was small, and I attended the local school until I was fifteen. Thankfully Mama kept in contact with Mr. and Mrs. York, Lady Kemsley's parents, and secured me a Season under the patronage of Harlow. I'll be forever grateful to her, even if nothing comes of my time here in London. I'll always remember it fondly, and you most of all."

Was it too soon to ask her to be his bride? Would she think he was rushing his decision and being hasty due to the physical desires they both encountered around each other?

But it was more than sexual cravings that kept him near Sophie. He trusted her, felt he could tell her everything, and she would willingly listen, debate, and offer an opinion. Not keep her thoughts from him merely because he was a duke and he ought to know all and what was best.

"But you seem to know Lord Carr. Their family has an estate near Highclere, I understand. How was it that you're associated with them?" Not that it mattered, but Lord Carr seemed to think he was acquainted enough with Sophie to single her out in town. And Henry had not missed the gentleman's interest in her at the previous events they attended. In fact, if he were to put a name to it, he would say Lord Carr was more interested than he ought to be since the gentleman was already married.

When did that stop married men from courting whom they wanted?

Well, Lord Carr would not have Sophie, and Henry would ensure that were the case.

"They do have a large estate not far from the town, and many of the young people I went to school with work as maids and footmen at the estate. But Mama would not allow me to apply, and certainly not after Harlow married Lord Kemsley. I know it sounds as if she was reaching above her means, but she only hoped better for me, I think. As I said before, I did act as a companion to the Dowager Viscountess Carr, but that was not every day." She paused, biting her lip in thought. "I agreed to a Season without any hopes, but I'm pleased to have met you. To be frank, I think you're lovely, and you kiss exquisitely well."

"Do I?" He moved his chair closer to Sophie's. He leaned toward her, almost nose to nose. "I came to London hoping to find a wife, a woman who shared my passions and was amenable to me, spirited even if I were fortunate. But I never thought I'd meet a woman that fired a hunger, a need that I fear will never be tamed. The thought of any men dancing with you, nevertheless marrying you, makes my stomach churn. I do not wish to share you with anyone."

She placed her palm against his cheek, and he read the understanding in her eyes. He was certain she felt the same as he. This could not just be him who was affected.

"I do not wish to share you with anyone else either."

"So perhaps we ought to promise that from today onward, we only dance with each other. That we supper together and not give anyone else any hope."

"I like that concept," she said, leaning forward and kissing him.

He reveled in the feel of her touch, her lips upon him. God damn it, she undid him. Made him want things he shouldn't, not in the garden of one of his friend's homes. They could not continue like this. He had to make a choice.

"Marry me, Sophie. I would not be here, kissing you, touching you, wanting to know everything about you if I were not desperate to make you mine."

Sophie's eyes went wide, and he could not adore her more. He supposed he may have surprised her, but he could not continue this way and not offer his hand, nor did he want to.

"Are you certain? I know we get along so very well, but I do not want you to ask out of gentlemanly honor. Please ask me because you cannot see yourself with anyone but me for the rest of your life, as I cannot," she stated, undoing him further.

He reached for her, pulling her to sit on his lap. She let out a delightful squeal but wrapped her arms around his neck, nestling against him. "We can keep this between us if you like for a day or so just so you can calm to the idea of becoming a duchess. But I'm not asking because of the passions we share. I'm asking because I do not want anyone but you as my duchess or the mother of my children. I'm in love with you, Sophie. I cannot think straight when we're apart. That is the truth of why I'm asking."

"Oh, Henry," she said, reaching for him and taking his lips. He lost himself in her arms, kissed her back with everything he had, and lost his heart, for better or worse.

Fourteen

S ophie could not remember a more delightful afternoon. They talked the hours away, laughed at silly antics from their childhood, and lost themselves in each other's arms. The afternoon slowly ebbed toward dusk, and she knew Henry had long overstayed the time Harlow had allowed them.

"I should leave," he sighed, leaning back on the daybed they had relaxed upon most of the afternoon. "But I must admit that I do not want to."

"Hmm, I could not agree more. I do not wish for you to go either, but Harlow will come looking for us if we dally any longer. However, I have had an idea I could put to you."

"Please do," he said, his lips brushing the side of her neck and eliciting a shiver down her spine. She bit her lip, losing the ability to think straight when he did such things to her. No matter what he said to deny the fact, Holland was a rogue and knew how to seduce a woman into his arms. Her especially.

"There is no ball this evening, no dinner parties to attend, and so I wondered if ..." Sophie questioned whether she should ask him what she was about to. She did not want him to think she was too brash, but nor did she not want to spend another moment without him. A whole evening without seeing Henry was too long to endure.

"Wondered what, Sophie?" He tilted her jaw and met her eyes.

"Your yard and Lord Kemsley's join you mentioned. Perhaps we could meet here later this evening. When everyone is abed?" Sophie bit her lip, holding her breath as she waited for Henry to answer. Would he say yes or no? Would he caution her about being so fast? No matter her past, this future with Henry was what she wanted, and no one would make her feel guilty for how she felt about him, how much she wanted him.

The man in her arms was her choice. Something she had never had before in her life. She was betrothed, weeks from marrying the man she loved. There was nothing wrong with wanting to see him as much as she could.

He nodded, a small smile playing about his lips and heat burning in his gaze. "I shall meet you here after midnight."

Sophie nodded. The time could not pass soon enough.

THEY PARTED NOT LONG AFTER THEIR agreement, and ignoring Harlow's pointed stares during dinner, Sophie managed to avoid too many prying questions from her cousin. She wanted to tell Harlow of the betrothal, that Henry was an honorable man and had done right by her, but she could not. The truth of her situation still did not seem real, and giving her a day or so to become used to the idea of her change in status and life, in general, was a gift that would not last long.

Henry would not go back on his word, and she would soon be ready to announce their happy news. Possibly even tomorrow, she would inform Henry he should speak to Kemsley and gain his permission to marry.

Sophie laid her napkin on the table and met Harlow's gaze. "Thank you for this afternoon and the lovely dinner. I must say I'm fatigued and think I shall retire early if you do not mind."

"Of course I do not mind, my dear. I think I shall be doing the same," Harlow said. "Do you still wish to go shopping tomorrow? I have an appointment with Madame Laurent. New gowns are the order of the day, and I would like them delivered before the end of the Season."

Sophie bit back a laugh at Lord Kemsley's raised brow at the mention of more dresses. She pushed back her chair, thanking a footman who helped her.

"I have not changed my mind about tomorrow. I'm looking forward to our outing," she said, smiling at Lord Kemsley.

He shook his head in resignation. "Well, when you ladies are off shopping, I shall be home, working and keeping the estates running as they should."

Harlow threw him a pointed stare. "Are you trying to say something, husband?" she asked.

"Not at all, my dear," he quipped, laughter shining in his eyes.

"Goodnight." Sophie smiled, leaving Harlow and her husband alone. They were so in love, so sweet in their teasing of each other. A union she longed to have herself, and now she would. With Henry.

Upon making her room, she requested a bath and soaked in the tub for longer than she ought if her crinkled fingers were anything to go by.

Her maid helped her dress into a clean shift and slipped on her dressing gown. She dismissed her for the night, wanting to ensure she was alone. Sophie snuffed the candles in her room and sat in the window, watching the back gardens and the pavilion she had agreed to meet Henry in later that evening.

It was already past ten, and the time would soon arrive when she would need to sneak out. The sounds of the servants closing up the house and settling down themselves soon quietened to silence. Sophie remained in the window, listening for any noise that may suggest anyone was still up, but after hearing nothing, she decided it was safe.

She tiptoed toward her door and, cracking it open just the slightest, looked out onto the long passageway for anyone she may have missed. The hall was cloaked in the moonlight, and she darted down the stairs, thankful the front footman was nowhere to be seen.

Sophie crept toward the back parlor and opened the glass doors, wary of making the tiniest sound as she stepped onto the terrace. Keeping to the shadows, she slipped into the gardens and ran the remainder of the way to the pavilion she had spent such a lovely afternoon in with Henry.

Her concerns that he would not be there were eradicated when slipping into the pavilion. She found him seated on the daybed, looking up at the ceiling as if he were watching the stars.

"You did come," she whispered, slowing her steps as she walked toward him.

He sat up, reaching for her when she came

close enough. "I said that I would, and anyway, bar sickness or death, there would be no reason as to why I would not meet you as agreed."

She ran her fingers through his dark locks, pushing them from his handsome face that watched her with such care, such hunger that her heart skipped a beat.

"We're being devilish," she admitted, hoping Harlow never found out what she had asked of the duke. Not that she had offered anything but to spend more time with him. But did he expect more from her this evening? She should have thought about that before asking to visit him again.

"What are you thinking?" he asked her, his hands sliding low on her back, so much so that his fingers brushed the top of her derrière.

"I'm fearful. Now that we're alone, I feel unsure suddenly," she admitted. Sophie took a calming breath. She was with Henry. He would not force her. He would not do anything that she did not want him to. She could trust him.

"I'll not push you toward anything you are not ready for, Sophie. If all we do this evening is spend more time together, that will be pleasure enough."

She slipped onto his lap, grateful he was so kind and good to her. "What a shame more gentlemen in London are not like you."

"I'm a patient man, and you've promised to

be mine. Why would I not want to give you everything you desire, even if that is time?"

"Well, I may wish for more than time. A kiss or two would be welcome." Her body warmed at the thought. "You make me feel so amazing, Henry. Being in your arms, being loved by you, is an ecstasy I never thought to enjoy."

He tumbled them onto the daybed cushions, and she laughed, stifling the sound with her hand. "Do not tickle me. I cannot contain myself when I'm fondled."

"Really?" He pinned her to the bed, unrelenting with his fingers as they tickled her waist. She squealed, laughing, trying to squirm away but to no avail. "Henry, please stop. Please," she begged him.

He did as she asked, and relief swamped her that he had listened to her and respected her enough to do so, even if they were only playing.

"You're not wearing many clothes, Sophie," he growled, leaning back to examine her person. Her dressing gown gaped, and even she could see her shift barely covered her decently. "Do you have any idea how desirable I find you? The moment I saw you, I knew our lives would be connected somehow."

"I'm glad that has come to be, too," she said, reaching for him.

He took her lips in a slow and unhurried kiss. A kiss that made her head spin. Their tongues tangled, and their bodies came together, his weight pressing against her. Sophie could feel his body, his hardness, Henry's wild, strong masculinity.

Her body burst to life, and she clung to him, wanting him with a need that surpassed any fear and trepidation that always lingered in her mind.

He did not move to do more, to propel them further than they had ever gone before. Her body longed, ached for his touch.

She pressed against his shoulders, rolling him onto his back. "I want to give you something," she said, kissing her way down his neck, chest, and stomach. "And you will let me." Her words brooked no argument. "You're so generous, and now I wish to be," she explained, hoping her act of brazenness did not fail as he had not failed her.

FIFTEEN

Henry relaxed onto the daybed. The seductive touch of Sophie, her kisses down his neck, and her nimble fingers on his body left him grappling for purchase. He'd never been touched by a woman in such a way, and not because he had not wanted to, but because he chose not to be like so many titled men in London. Like his own errant father had been.

Sophie deserved to know he was not the rogue he pretended to be and was as innocent as she. "Sophie," he said, clasping her hand against his chest and pulling her back to lay beside him. "There is something that you must know before we do anything further. A secret I've kept from others but one I do not wish to keep from you."

She settled next to him, giving him her full attention, and he knew he could not back down now. The truth needed to be told, and he was certain she would only be pleased by what he conveyed.

"What is it?" she asked him as he fumbled to find the words.

"Well, as you know, many rumors circulate around town about me. The most common that I'm a rogue, a rake with a different woman in my bed every week. Shamefully I've allowed those rumors to circulate and thrive, never doing anything to stem the lies. But I wanted you to know that they are untruths and that I'm nothing like I'm depicted."

She leaned up on her elbow, a small frown between her brows. "Truly? But why is such a thing said about you if you say they are not what is happening? Surely such rumors started from some truth?"

He hated that she did not believe him, that the *ton* and their wayward tittering always made people out worse than what they were. "I'm not a rake, far from it. I can only assume the slur was placed upon me because my father was far from exemplary. He had many mistresses during his marriage to my mother, and the *ton*, I suppose, think the apple does not fall far from the tree. But I'm not like my father, and although during my first Season in town, I drank and danced and followed quite a wild bunch of men about the city, I never once felt the need, the desire to go any further than a few stolen kisses with the lasses ... until now that is."

Her mouth opened as if she were going to say something before she closed it with a snap. "Are you trying to tell me you've never been with a woman before, Henry?"

The horror that twisted her features made his stomach churn. Did she think him so green that he would not know how to satisfy her in such a way? He nodded, not wanting any secrets between them. "I am, yes. Until I met you, I had not wanted to be with a woman so intimately, but just being in your presence, catching a glimpse of you across a ballroom floor, and I'm done. I am yours, Sophie. I want you in my bed, as my wife, and only you."

Her eyes went wide, and he wondered what she was thinking. At times she was so hard to read that he was never sure what went on in that smart mind of hers.

"Henry ..." She blew out a muddled breath. "How can this be?" She shook her head, clearly unable to acknowledge what he was telling her. He supposed it would be hard to consider such a truth. Especially since so many women gossiped about him as if they had been lovers with him themselves.

He had not missed some of the triumphant looks from married ladies, the sly glances and whispered words when he had danced with them at a previous ball that seemed to permit them to, in their own silly minds, say they had become lovers.

All untrue and fabricated, and he should have stopped such fanciful rumors, but he had not. They protected him from having to explain why he had not rutted his way around London.

Not until he had seen Sophie had he thanked God he had not succumbed, because he only wanted to surrender to her.

"On my life, I swear it is true. You are the only woman I want, and upon meeting you, I knew we would one day be here. I'm in love with you, and I want only you. I do not need any other to warm my bed."

She bit her lip, leaning forward before kissing him. He clasped her cheek, deepening the kiss and showing her without words what she meant to him.

Everything.

SOPHIE FOUGHT TO SETTLE HER MIND, TO stop her stomach from twisting into nervous knots.

Henry was a virgin!

How was that possible? Well, she knew how it was, he had explained it to her, but still, it did not seem real. A virile, handsome, sweet man like he was could not have not succumbed to women.

The thought that he had never been with anyone else, nor did he want to until her ... Satisfaction thrummed through her that he was hers, truly and in all ways. No one else had lain with him, been so intimate of the body with him.

Pity you could not say the same, Sophie.

She cast the horrid thought aside. In her mind, she was still a young woman, full of dreams and hopes. Not bruised and battered from her one horrible night with Lord Carr. She would not allow the past to dampen what a glorious future she could have with Henry.

He need never know her shame, and to replace the memory that she carried with something extraordinary, warm, and full of love was a temptation too strong to ignore. She would be with him, marry him, and be his lover, his wife, and never look back to dwell on the cold, horrid past.

But that was not honest, and no marriage should start on a bed of untruths. But how to tell Holland of her past without ruining her future?

"It is the same for me," she fibbed, torn between keeping the truth hidden from him or laying herself bare. She slid her hand over his chest. His heart beat fast under her palm, but she did not relent. He gifted her so much pleasure at the theater the other evening. It was only fair she did the same for him.

Her hand left his taut stomach and slipped over his hardened manhood. So large and jutting through his breeches. She stroked him through the soft cloth, tightening her fingers around his girth.

He sucked in a breath, closing his eyes in satisfaction. His enjoyment sparked a desire to do more.

She flicked open the buttons on his falls, his manhood breaking free of his breeches. She clasped him, holding his wide girth, and stroked him as he had stroked her. She had never been so bold with a man or touched a man so freely, but she wanted to with Henry.

She wanted to give him everything. Make him feel as wonderful as he made her, not just in pleasure but when they were alone, just as they were now.

He pressed into her hand, and she stroked his rigid flesh. She glanced down at him in her hand, his manhood so soft but with a rod of iron running through it.

She marveled at him, wondering what he would feel like within her. Fear curdled in her stomach at the thought, but she pushed it away. Henry was not Lord Carr. He was nothing like that satyr of a man.

She stroked him and cupped his baubles before taking him in hand yet again. She reveled in his sighs of delight, his glassy, heavy-lidded eyes that watched her every touch.

"Do you like that, Your Grace?" she cooed, leaning over him so she could kiss him.

He nodded, reaching for her. They came together, their mouths fused, their tongues twisting in delight as she played with him. He groaned in her mouth, the most erotic moment of her life, and heat pooled at her core.

She ached for his touch, wanting to feel as incredible as he now did.

His hand covered hers, guiding her, tightening on his cock, and she grinned. "Next time, I'll know what you like."

"I like you and your hand more than anything." The breath of his words tickled her cheek, and she giggled.

"God, Sophie," he moaned as hot liquid spilled over her hand and his shirt. "I want you so much."

"I want you too, but not here, not this night. Tonight I wanted you to have the pleasure you afforded me. But there will be more nights, Henry. Many more."

He nodded, pulling her against his side. "I have a meeting with Kemsley tomorrow, and I'll be asking for your hand, and after the banns are called, you shall be mine within a month."

She snuggled into his warm, virile body. "The

month cannot end soon enough. I love you if I have not said it before."

He glanced down at her, affection filling his brown eyes. "You had not said it before, and it pleases me that you do. I love you too," he said before kissing her senseless yet again.

She could well get used to such affection.

Sixteen

Henry knocked on the Kemsley's London town house door and waited for the footman to answer. He did not have to wait long before the servant promptly welcomed him inside.

"I'm here to see Lord Kemsley," he mentioned, handing the footman his card. He wanted everything as it should be before asking for Sophie's hand. Should any other gentleman offer for her, they would do the same, and so he would leave nothing to chance.

"Right this way, Your Grace," the footman said, leading him toward the library.

"The Duke of Holland to see you, my lord."

Kemsley looked up as his footman introduced him. "Holland, good of you to call. I hoped to catch up with you today, but you have saved me a brisk walk." He turned to the footman. "Thank you, Peter. Please close the door. We're not to be disturbed," Kemsley ordered.

"Take a seat," Kemsley continued, gesturing to the chair across from the desk. Henry settled himself in the comfortable leather, oddly nervous to ask for Kemsley's approval to marry the woman he loved.

"I suppose you're here to make amends," Kemsley said, catching Henry off guard.

His blood ran cold, and for a horrific moment, he thought the earl may have known of Sophie and his rendezvous in the garden the night before.

"Make amends?" he questioned, hoping to be mistaken but not seeing how he could be.

Kemsley studied him, and Henry fought not to squirm. "Last evening, I visited Whites and found a disturbing name in the betting book. I'm curious why you would put your name to such a bet and commit the heinous act of pretending to like Sophie when it is clear you do not."

Blast it all to hell. Henry fisted his hands in his lap and fought to release them, to clear his mind and not act hasty with his reaction to such a lie. He reminded himself Kemsley did not know his true feelings, which had nothing to do with the bet.

"You are correct, I did put my name to the betting book, but after meeting Miss York, I forgot all about the wager and merely wished to spend time with her. I'm not courting her to win one thousand pounds. I can assure you of that."

Kemsley watched him, his eyes hard and considering his words. "You were foolish to scribble your name. Many wish to win, as you know, and may see that your affections for Miss York are insincere and wish to make trouble for you."

The thought horrified him. Such slander would injure Sophie, and he could not bear for that to happen. "Why would anyone do such a thing?" Henry argued. "I have no enemies and wish for no trouble."

"That does not mean others do not wish to make the Season a little livelier with scandal and upset. A hurt Miss York would feel should she learn she's part of a bet to which you put your name."

Henry sighed. "I tried to remove myself, but Lord Bankes would not hear of it. Something about the club's rules, but I promise you, this is not why I called today. Please do not say anything to Miss York. It will only upset her, and there is no reason why she should know."

Kemsley narrowed his eyes, and Henry could see he was not convinced. "Why did you come today?"

"I came to ask for your approval to marry Miss York. I want Sophie to be my wife. To be the next Duchess of Holland."

Kemsley's eyes widened, and for a moment,

Henry thought he'd shocked him mute. "The great Holland bachelor era is over. How the ladies will need their smelling salts when they hear such lamentable news."

Henry shrugged. If only Kemsley knew the truth, but then at least Sophie did, and she was the only one who needed to know his secret. A riddle she would keep.

"I would not say it was ever so great, but the future, I believe, shall be. I shall marry a woman I love, and I do love Sophie more than I thought possible. She makes me laugh, is sweet and kind, and everything right in the world, and I look forward to making her mine."

Kemsley nodded, taking in his words and losing a little of the annoyance in his gaze. "I'm happy to hear this, Holland. Miss York is, as you say, an honest and loyal woman who will complement the Holland line. I do not think you could have chosen better for yourself. Not that I'm biased or anything toward her family."

Henry laughed, pleased they would be related going forward, if only distantly and through their wives. "I have asked Sophie to marry me, and she has said yes, but I wanted to get your approval and that of her mama, whom I understand you're in contact with, before announcing it publicly."

"I am indeed. I shall write to Mrs. York today with the good news. She will be pleased for her daughter and will want to travel to London to celebrate with you both. Once I have heard back from her, we shall announce it in the paper."

"That would be most pleasant," Henry said. "I will have my steward forward all the contracts to you to look over, and we shall discuss the matter further in the coming weeks." Henry stood, holding out his hand.

Kemsley took it, shaking it with a firm grip. "Welcome to the family and to the married club. I think you'll find it to your liking."

Henry shook his hand back. "Oh, I know I shall find it so." He paused. "And the bet, will you agree to keep it between us? I am sorry for my error of judgment, but I meant no disrespect or harm to Sophie. I would never wish that for her. She is my life now."

"I shall keep the secret, even from my darling wife, but I would suggest trying to rid your name of the book as soon as possible. As I said, with the announcement of your betrothal forthcoming, society loves trouble, and a duke marrying a woman of little means who took part in a bet to win her hand, well ... should Sophie hear of it, I'm not certain she will ever forgive you."

The idea made his stomach churn. He could not lose her now. Not when they were so close to being married. "I shall amend the book, even if I have to sneak into Whites in the middle of the night to do so."

"Good man. Now, let us toast this happy occasion."

"Pour away," Henry said, thinking of when he would travel to Whites to remove the bet from prying eyes that could undo everything he had built with the woman he loves.

Sophie.

A WEEK LATER, SOPHIE ATTENDED LORD and Lady Astor's ball. One that was held yearly in their opulent gardens that overlooked the Thames. The night was balmy and warm, with not a breath of wind or cloud in the sky, giving those in attendance a wonderful view of the stars.

"Miss York," a masculine voice called along with a waving hand through the crush of guests in attendance, although she could not see exactly who reached out to her.

Sophie had lost sight of Harlow and Lord Kemsley and was slowly making her way about the gardens in search of them. Maybe they had taken a punt on the Thames. An adventure guests could take part in if they wished.

"Miss York," somebody called again, this time close enough that she recognized the voice. She hastened her steps in the opposite direction to the man who advanced, but not quickly enough. A hand reached out and clasped her arm, pulling her to a stop.

She wrenched herself free, turning to glare at Lord Carr. How dare he put his hands on her. The man was far too presumptuous for his own good. "Do not touch me, Lord Carr," she ordered, scowling at the man who had caused her so much pain. Why he thought she even wished to see his face was beyond her. Every time she did so, it filled her with terror and disgust.

"I wish to introduce you to my wife, Lady Carr," he said waving his wife over to join them, his tone one of gaiety as if he had not read at all or understood her loathing of him. "I feel our last meeting was too short-lived to do so." She had no reason to be afraid of this man anymore. He could not hurt her now. Not with Harlow and Lord Kemsley keeping her safe and the love of Henry.

"Lady Carr," she said, dipping into a curtsy when she finally joined them. "It has been some years since we met last," she said, attempting to be polite to the woman who no doubt suffered much being married to the fiend who was his lordship.

"Yes, I do remember you. Miss York, you attended our engagement ball and sat with Carr's grandmother all night. A shame for you not to take part in the society that visited Highclere that evening. A woman in your situation would not enjoy such luxury or good conversation often. Not until now, at least."

"Oh yes, she is the cousin to Lady Kemsley, my dear. Much amenity nowadays, I should imagine. You have been spoiled, Miss York," Lord Carr said, his tone one of condescension, as if she did not deserve to remove herself from the poverty in which she grew up.

Sophie studied his lordship, wanting to scratch his cruel eyes from his head. "I shall pass on your thoughts to Lord and Lady Kemsley of my overindulgence here in London. Maybe they will agree that I ought not to rise above my station." There, she had defended herself. The shock on Lord and Lady Carr's features was comical, and satisfaction thrummed through her.

Lord Carr cleared his throat, his mouth pinching into a displeased line. "And now we hear you're to marry Holland. What a triumph, Miss York," his lordship murmured. "Tell us both what was it that won you to him. What favors did you perform? We must know all."

SEVENTEEN

"I think what is between a husband and wife, or in our case, my betrothed and myself, is private, Lord Carr. I would suggest you refrain from asking such a pointed and ill-placed question again toward my future wife," Holland said, coming to stand at Sophie's side.

How dare the viscount be so impertinent. The gentleman ought to know better and know his place. He took her hand and placed it on his arm, covering her trembling fingers with his lest the inappropriate Lord Carr thought to continue asking such inquiries that he had no right knowing the answer to in the first place.

Whatever was wrong with the man?

"My apologies, Your Grace. We're old friends, you see. I did not think the question out of place at all, merely the kind of fun banter that Miss

York and myself once shared," his lordship stated in the way of excuse.

Henry was not buying his pretty words for one moment. There was something about Carr that he did not like. If he were to describe it, a falseness, a meanness, that did not sit well with him. His lordship's wife, whose gaze was cold enough to freeze the Thames, stood beside him, her endorsement of the unsuitable question clear to see.

Well, he would not allow either of them to ask any further queries. Old friends from the same county or not, their time together this evening was over.

"If you will excuse us. I wish to dance with my fiancée." Without waiting for a reply, Henry escorted Sophie onto the dance floor and pulled her into his arms, relishing the feel of her in his embrace once more.

"I do not like Lord Carr," he stated, glaring at the smirking fob over Sophie's shoulder.

"Then that would make two of us." She reached up and discreetly led his attention back to her instead. The urge to pummel Lord Carr into a pulp rode him hard. How dare he ask Sophie how it was that she had captured his heart.

"Do not think any more of the viscount. He has always been too familiar and too sure of himself. That has not changed in all the years I have known him, not even when he is before a duke and ought to know better."

Henry pulled her close, having missed her these past two days. They were betrothed, after all. No one could say anything about how familiar they were to one another now. Nor should they dare. "How long has it been since you've spoken to Lord Carr? I would think it was not long enough."

Sophie chuckled at his words, and he drank in the sound, enjoying her laughter and happiness. "Not since I was fifteen. A long time ago."

"What a shame he has come to London. Some people ought to remain in the past and the country."

"I could not agree more," she murmured, a shadow clouding her eyes before she blinked, and it was gone. "You're my future now. And I, for one, cannot wait to be your wife. To be together always, to return home after nights such as this. Alone ..." She grinned.

The idea made him inwardly groan, and he fought to keep control of his person. She was too tempting for her own good. Did she not know what a temptress she was to his soul? How much she consumed his every thought?

"The idea of being alone with you now is compelling beyond reason. Do you think we could sneak away?" he asked, looking about and seeing no one was taking much notice of them in any case.

"Perhaps I have a headache and require assistance to return home," she suggested. "Now that we're engaged, I'm sure Harlow will allow your aid."

He smirked and halted their dance. Looking about the room, he spied Lord and Lady Kemsley and hastily started toward them.

"What are you doing?" she asked, close to his heels.

"As you asked and as I said, your every whim and desire is mine to fulfill, and if you have a megrim, then I wish to take you home so you may feel better."

"You're incorrigible," she breathed just as they came before her cousin and Kemsley.

SOPHIE WATCHED WITH ADMIRATION AS, with a well-crafted excuse and not a lot of persuasions, Harlow and Lord Kemsley allowed Henry to take her home for them since she was suffering from a terrible headache and needed a tisane immediately.

It did not take them long before they were ensconced in the ducal Holland carriage and making their way through Mayfair streets. Sophie settled into the plush, leather-lined carriage seats, so much nicer than any she had ever traveled in before. Even Harlow's family carriage was not as lovely as Henry's seemed to be.

She looked about and noted the curtains matched the upholstery on the unusually wide seats. "Your carriage is lovely, Henry. I do not think I've ever traveled in such finery," she said, watching him settle on the squabs across from her.

"You should become accustomed to my way of life, my darling, for I intend to spoil you and gift all you desire."

The word desire reverberated in her mind, and she could not deny that she liked to hear him state such things, for she, too, only wanted to please and love him as he deserved.

She reached over and untied the little knots that held the curtains open and slowly closed them all, enclosing them in a shadowed, secluded space. Sophie moved to sit beside Henry, leaning up to kiss the underside of his ear. He smelled divine, of sandalwood and spice. "Order the carriage driver to drive around a little while, Your Grace," she suggested in a tone she hoped was as seductive as she felt.

He barked out the order immediately, startling her. "What do you have planned for us?" he asked. He moaned when she kissed his neck, small, soft brushes of her lips against his skin.

Before she could answer, he turned and picked her up, settling her on his lap. But unlike before, she did not sit on his knees. Instead, she straddled his legs, leaving her exposed.

Heat kissed her skin, and hunger licked along her spine. "I want you," she admitted, having never felt the burning desire that coursed through her right at that moment.

His eyes darkened, burned with a need that matched hers, and he kissed her, took her lips in a kiss that left her reeling, breathless, and wanting more.

So much more.

His hands fumbled with her dress, and cool air kissed her legs, her thighs before she moaned when his hand slipped against her cunny, rubbing her, teasing her aching flesh.

She moaned and held his shoulders to steady herself as his touch teased her to within a stroke of release.

"You're so wet, Sophie. So delicious." He met her eyes in the darkness, and she knew the time had come. They could not continue to tease each other in such a way. They were engaged now, and she wanted him in all ways.

She could trust Henry. He was everything to her, including her heart.

Sophie reached for his falls, ripping his breeches open. His manhood sprung into her hand, and she stroked him, long and slow. He moaned, the torture in his voice. The need made her want him even more.

"You're so hard," she rasped breathlessly, positioning herself above him, his cock at her core.

"Sophie, wait," he cautioned. "You're a maid. I don't want to hurt you." His hands stilled her actions, stopping her from doing what she wanted. What they both wanted.

"You are worth the discomfort," she said, hoping that with Henry there would be no pain, only pleasure. His grip eased and with care, she lowered herself onto him, reminding herself that this was Henry. She was in control. She could stop at any moment. That this was what she wanted. He was whom she loved.

He leaned back against the squabs, watching her. Ecstasy and satisfaction washed over his features as she settled upon him. He was large, thicker than she expected, but so good. He filled and inflamed her body, and the urge to enjoy the gift that was her betrothed was too much.

She lifted herself and came down upon him with caution, but there was no pain, no burning or hard, distressing grips upon her person. He held her hips with care, guiding her, allowing her to set her own pace.

He was an elixir of satisfaction and peace she could not get enough of.

"Henry," she gasped, riding him, taking him deep. He groaned, thrusting into her, teasing her with every stroke. "I cannot wait to be yours."

"You already are mine," his low voice declared

with promise. He wrapped his arms around her, lifting her off the seat and promptly laying her onto the squabs.

The soft cushions cocooned her as he came over her. He thrust into her, hard and with demanding strokes. Sophie wrapped her legs around his hips, content to enjoy this marvelous gift they gave each other.

She clasped his face, pulling him down for a kiss, and gasped as tremors thrummed through her unlike anything she'd ever known, and then pleasure exploded through her body, out from her core to send bliss through the rest of her person.

"Henry," she gasped through his kiss. Warmth filled her core, his release blending with hers. He did not stop until the final tremors subsided to blissful oblivion.

He came to lay beside her, pulling her into his arms. "That was wonderous," he stated, kissing her temple.

She huddled into his muscled chest, their legs still entwined. "I adore you," she whispered.

"And I cherish you, and now I think more than anything we require to be married sooner rather than in a month. That will be too long to have you in my bed."

"We cannot elope," she said, fear curdling a little of her ecstasy. "People will think badly of our union and that it is not what you wish."

He frowned, shaking his head. "No, we will not elope, but I shall gain a special license, and before the week is out, you shall be my duchess."

Sophie sighed, preferring this idea above anything else. "I would indeed like that to be the case."

"As would I."

EIGHTEEN

As promised, they were married in St George's on Hanover Square—the parish church of Mayfair—three days later. Thankfully Sophie's mama and closest friends were in attendance. Her cousin Lila—now Lady Billington—too returned from the country to attend and enjoy the last few weeks of the Season.

She stood beside Henry at the wedding breakfast in the gardens of his London estate. A chilled glass of champagne in hand, she marveled at how lucky she was to marry the man she adored and loved and he in return.

How was it she was now the Duchess of Holland? But when several friends dipped into a curtsy and greeted her by her title, only then did the reality of her life start to seem factual.

"Are you happy?" Henry asked, lifting her

hand and softly kissing the top of her gloved fingers.

She smiled up at him, unable to hide the day's delight. "I'm so very happy, Henry. I do not think the day could be any more perfect." To her surprise and without any care for what anyone thought, Henry closed the space between them and kissed her. She leaned into the embrace, her body yearning for his touch. Not seeing him the last two days leading up to their nuptials had seemed an eternity.

He was everything to her. Offered his hand and married her as he promised he would. A dream beyond her reach, and yet, as real as she was standing in the Holland gardens, she was now his wife. Safe from harm, the powerful man at her side no one, not even Lord Carr, would cross.

The morning was perfection personified, and this evening promised to be even more entertaining. They were to hold their first London ball as a married couple. Although the celebration was primarily to honor their marriage, it was an excellent way to introduce her to the *ton* as the new Duchess of Holland, if nothing else.

All their guests were well on the way to being foxed by luncheon. Without saying a word, Henry escorted her into her new home, a large Georgian manor that she had not visited before this day. He introduced her to the staff, paying particular attention to the housekeeper and her lady's maid.

"Shall we retire for a time, my dear?" he asked, raising his brows as he led her toward the stairs. "I think you shall love your suite of rooms."

A thrill ran through her that she would have her own suite of rooms. She had never had anything so grand before in her life. "Are my rooms near yours?" she asked, hoping they were not too far apart.

He shook his head, smiling. "I would not have it any other way." They came to the first-floor landing and turned left along the corridor. "This is your bedchamber, my darling," Henry explained.

Sophie stepped into a large, rectangular room that housed two marble fireplaces. Not one, but two! The windows overlooked the back gardens and terrace, and in the distance, she could see the sphere of St Paul's Cathedral.

The bedding was a dusty pink and very pretty. A large, four-poster bed against one wall, the dark mahogany wood suiting the lighter shades of the bedding and matching upholstered settee situated before the fire.

"Henry, this is stunning," she sighed, moving about the room, unable to hide the excitement that flooded her. To have this as her sanctuary, her home from this day forward, was a blessing she could never have foretold.

She sat on the dressing table chair, taking in her meager hairbrush and the paste jewelry she owned that the maid had unpacked and laid out for her.

Henry came to stand behind her, his eyes meeting her in the reflection. "There is a bellpull beside the fire should you require your maid or anything else. And if you come through this door," Henry said, walking over to a panel on the wall she had not noticed. "And press here," he demonstrated, "it opens a hidden door that leads into my bedchamber."

Sophie joined Henry at the door, slipping past him and into his chamber, which was a mirror image of hers, except where hers was feminine, his was masculine. Dark-emerald bedding and window dressings with dark-green silk wallpaper would leave no one in doubt who slept there. A duke, a powerful man.

Her husband.

"And I can come in here whenever I please?" She grinned at the amusement in his eyes at her question.

"Of course. In fact, I have a surprise for you."

Sophie looked about the room but could not see any flowers or champagne to toast their union privately. She looked at him curiously as to what it was. "A surprise? Where?" she asked.

He reached out and clasped her hand, pulling her back into her suite of rooms and walking her to the opposite side, where another hidden door was masked as paneling.

"In here," he said.

Sophie entered the room, half the size of her bedchamber, and gasped. A bathing room. A large bath filled with steaming water sat before an unlit hearth. A cupboard full of linens and a small table held various soaps and fresh herbs. The room smelled divine, not to mention the bath looked utterly decadent right at this moment.

"I did not know what you liked best, so I ordered the housekeeper to purchase a variety of soap scents for you to enjoy."

Sophie glanced at the water, and already she longed to slip into the bath and relax after such a busy and exciting morning.

"Why do I feel as though you're going to indulge me, Henry?" She went to him, leaning up and wrapping her arms around his neck. She stole a kiss, reveling in the feel of his hands coming about her waist and holding her firm.

"Because I will be." He grinned and then, without a word, let her go and spun her about. He made light work of the buttons on her gown, sending a shiver down her spine when he kissed the back of her neck. Sophie bit her lip, impatient for what was to come.

"Shall we bathe together?" He asked as her gown dropped to the floor to pool at her feet.

She nodded, glancing over her shoulder. "Untie my stays. A bath sounds heavenly."

He did as she asked before he started on his own attire. He ripped his shirt from his breeches, hoisting it over his head and throwing it aside. He kicked off his boots, shoved his breeches down, and, heaven forbid, stood before her as naked as the day he was born.

Her mouth dried at the sight of him. His muscular body, broad shoulders, and heavy-lidded eyes that burned with need made her body tremble in awareness. His chest rose and fell with every breath, and his stomach had a delightful V that led to satisfaction.

Sophie kicked off her slippers, hoisting her shift from her person, wanting nothing between them. With a little devil on her shoulder, she lifted her leg onto the bath and slowly slid her silk stocking down, meeting Henry's hungry gaze that watched her every move.

A muscle worked in his jaw, and expectation pooled heat between her legs. Unheeded by modesty, Sophie stepped into the bath and sank under the scented water, watching Henry join her. His cock jutted out before him, thick and rigid, and she swallowed, her body craving him like air.

He sat across from her, watching her with determined silence.

"This is divine. I cannot thank you enough for today, Henry," she quipped, ignoring the hunger that burned between them. "It has exceeded all my expectations and has been the best of my life."

As quick as a wink, he reached for her, pulling her to sit between his legs. His hands slipped over her stomach, holding her close before he reached for a cake of soap, lathering it between his palms.

"I shall never forget today either, Sophie." His hands settled on her body, washing her, stroking her. His fingers circled her nipples, bringing them to tightened, circular beads. She closed her eyes, reveling in his touch, her willing body ready for whatever he wanted to do.

"From almost the very first moment we spoke, I've wanted you."

"Mmm," she agreed. "I'm so delighted we're the same on that score. From the first day I saw you at the Derby's ball, I've been curious about you too. How lucky we are to have been introduced."

His grin turned wicked as his hand slipped between her legs to stroke her cunny. Sophie spread her legs, wanting his touch there. His fingers worked her body, teasing her, and she moaned, craving release.

"You're so beautiful. I'm going to make you come so hard, my darling, that I will finally hear you scream my name."

His dirty words, ones she never thought to

hear a duke utter, almost undid her. She turned in his arms, breast to chest, enjoying the slippery hold they had on each other.

"Promise?" she goaded.

He narrowed his eyes, determination burning in his dark depths. "You do not believe me?"

She shrugged, enjoying the game they played. "Maybe. Only time will tell."

He took her lips in a searing kiss, stealing her breath. "The time is now," he declared, kissing her again and proving that, indeed, he was in earnest.

NINETEEN

enry clasped Sophie by the hips and guided her upon him. His cods tightened at the exquisite sensation of Sophie in his arms, his wife and love. She sighed, a most delectable sound that ignited a fire in his veins, and he thrust into her, needing her, wanting to sate her every desire and wish.

She did not pull away from the madness she dragged forth in him. She rocked against him, taking what she wanted, owning her pleasure with every rise of her sweet derrière. Her fingers tightened painfully in his hair, but he enjoyed it, wanted her to be as mad with pleasure as he was.

He groaned, wanting to consume her, be more than he ever could. He wished he had met her sooner, that she had come to town when so many other debutantes did at eighteen. They could have been married years ago if that were the case.

He could not adore her more if he tried.

He would never understand how he had tumbled so hard and fast for her heart, but he had. There was something about his wife, his duchess, that completed him. She was his friend, the future mother of his children, the new matriarch of the great Holland name.

Maybe even today, on their wedding day, they may be so blessed to start a family.

"Henry!" She rocked against him, her breasts teasing his chest.

He slid his tongue up her neck, wanting to taste her and suckle the sensitive spot beneath her ear. She moaned, tipping her head in acquiescence. He clasped her under her arms, wrenching her down upon him, taking her, fucking her as they both enjoyed.

"I love screwing you," he admitted crudely.

She met his eyes, hers alight with understanding. "I like you screwing me, too," she mimicked wickedly.

Their tupping became frantic, and yet it wasn't enough. He wanted her more. He needed her out of this bath and on his bed. "I want to make you scream on our marriage bed."

She nodded, moving off him. He stood and reached for her, swooping her into his arms, and stepped out of the tub. She squealed, looking about them as the water splashed all over the floor.

"Henry, the water is going everywhere." She giggled as he ignored the mess and continued toward his room.

"That does not signify. There are other things I wish to do to you, and the bath is not big enough to satisfy my every desire."

Her eyes blazed with expectation. "Oh, that does sound intriguing. Would you elaborate on what you will do to me, husband?" Her voice had a sultry edge that hardened his cock to almost painful.

She would soon find out. He had wanted to taste her for some time. And he would. He threw her onto her bed, smiling as she bounced atop the linen.

"Lay back upon the bedding, duchess. I'm going to taste your quim, lick your sweet flesh until you're begging me to fuck you."

Her mouth opened in the most delicious way, and he leaned forward, stealing a kiss, before pushing against her shoulder to do as he asked. She lay back, watching him under hooded eyes before he clasped her ankles and pulled her to the side of the bed.

She yelped and giggled but allowed him his way. Henry slipped her legs over his shoulders and kissed his way along them. They were long and slim, perfect for wrapping about his body in the throes of pleasure.

He licked the water from her skin as he kissed

his way toward her notch. She dropped her knees open, revealing her sweet, pink flesh to his view. So perfect. He licked his lips, his mouth salivating at the thought of sampling her.

The first taste of her cunny rocked him to his core. She tasted of lilies, roses, and every other scented flower he knew to name. He closed his eyes, wanting to remember this moment for the rest of his life.

He had never been so intimate with a woman, but already she mewled, squirmed under his tutelage, and he understood that she enjoyed what he did.

The idea made him harder still, and he suckled her flesh, working her, continuing particular little strokes when she moaned. "You like that, Sophie. You like me licking your quim."

"Yes, I like it." Her voice, breathless, was like a Siren's call. He ran his thumb across her flesh, playing with the beaded nubbin that protruded at his touch.

She gasped. "Take me with your fingers, Henry," she begged. He needed no further instruction. He slipped one and then two fingers into her wet core and licked her engorged flesh while he fucked her with his hands.

She moaned, her fingers spiking into his hair, pulling him against her. Her body undulated, worked against his mouth, and he groaned, enjoying her delight.

She trembled under him, and he knew she was close. "Henry," she gasped. Do not stop. Please, do not stop," she begged, riding him as if he were taking her with his manhood.

He gave her what she wanted. What they both wanted and he felt the first tremors of her orgasm as it ripped through her core and she tightened about his fingers.

"Henry," she screamed, holding him against her until her pleasure reduced.

With one last kiss to her pinkened, satisfied flesh, he crawled up to lean over the top of her. "Did you appreciate my endeavor, Duchess?"

She nodded, her eyes heavy with satisfaction. "Oh yes, I did, Duke, and now you'll enjoy your turn just as much."

Without another word, she pushed against his shoulder, and he collapsed beside her. She straddled him, and kissed her way down his chest, paying particular attention to his nipples with little kisses before paying homage lower still.

"What are you going to do?" he asked her, hopeful but unwilling to ask outright for what he imagined.

"I'm going to do what you just did to me. Give you so much pleasure that you'll never look anywhere else but toward me from this day forward."

He smiled. Knowing no sexual act was required for that. He was smitten.

In love, unfashionably, with his wife.

TWENTY

S ophie had no clue what she was doing or how to continue what she had started. She kissed her way down Henry's stomach. His strong, muscular frame brought a smile to her lips, and she nibbled and teased him the further she delved.

How she adored him.

Before meeting Henry, she had not imagined men of nobility could be so striking. Indeed, Lord Carr, the only gentleman she knew growing up, was lean and gangly, with very little substance to him except his brute force when he wanted his way.

Henry's manhood jutted against her stomach, and she shifted to look at it, to study what she had never seen so clearly before. A little trepidation thrummed through her of taking him into her mouth. Could such a position even work?

He was larger this close, wider too. And yet,

still, she wanted to gift him the pleasure he had bestowed upon her. Surely the concept worked both ways. Determined to succeed, she wrapped her fingers about his length, stroking him, and watched with amazement as a little bead of pearl-colored liquid pooled at his manhood's opening.

She leaned forward, tasting it. The texture was odd, the liquid salty.

"Deuce, take me, Sophie. You're going to kill me," Henry groaned, leaning on one arm and watching her with hunger-filled eyes.

She grinned, happy that he liked what she was doing so far.

She licked him again, bolder this time, stroked the top of his cock with her tongue before taking him into her mouth.

As well as she could, she suckled him, stroked him, and mimicked what she hoped was correct. She really ought to have studied some of the naughty books Lord Kemsley thought were hidden in his library before she embarked on seducing her husband. At least then, she would know if she was doing this right.

"That feels so damn good." His fingers curled in her hair, holding her against him. "Do not stop sucking me. I want to come in your mouth."

His words pooled heat between her legs, and she drew them together, wanting him yet again. Sophie worked his manhood, licked the engorged vein that ran his length, teased, and did everything she believed pleased him.

His bottom lifted off the bed, grinding into her mouth, mimicking sex. He groaned, a sound of contentment, of need that left her euphoric and powerful. More mighty and in control than ever in her life.

"Don't stop, my love." His body thrust harder, quicker, into her mouth.

She did everything to keep her rhythm. The vein on his manhood pulsated against her tongue before warm liquid burst into her mouth. She fought to swallow his pleasure, sucking him until she was sure his satisfaction had ceased.

She kissed her way up his body before nestling at his side. "Did you enjoy that, Your Grace?" she asked.

He sighed, chuckling at the question she already knew the answer to. "You know that I did. Blast it, Sophie. How are we to attend our ball this evening when I feel like doing nothing but making love to you all evening?"

"Hosting our first ball on our wedding day was probably not as good an idea as I thought it would be. But do not worry, we have the rest of our lives to enjoy such evenings."

"And I presume we're both very much satisfied this afternoon. A ball will be a reprieve for an hour or two."

Sophie laughed. "An hour or two. I do believe the ball will last longer than that. But at least we can leave together now, and no one can say a word about it."

He dipped his head and kissed her on the top of her head. "That time will be the highlight of the night for me."

Sophie did not reply but knew it would be the highlight for her too.

THE EVENING WENT OFF WITHOUT A hitch, and Henry was happy for his new bride, who stood with Lady Kemsley and Lady Billington across the ballroom. All the ladies held champagne in their hands and appeared rosy-cheeked and lively as they discussed whatever it was that ladies debated.

A smile lifted Henry's lips, and he was unable to factor in how he had met and fallen headlong in love with a woman and was now a married man. Of course, he had always hoped to find a wife this Season, but the love, the devotion Sophie brought forth in him was beyond anything he had ever hoped for.

"I must offer you my congratulations, Your Grace. You must be thrilled with your choice of bride."

The uninvited voice of Lord Carr caught Henry by surprise, and he spun about, glaring at the man he knew had not been on the invitation list. There was something about Carr he did not like or trust. That he was here when he ought not to be only doubled his suspicions of him.

"Thank you," he said, willing to let his being here go for the moment, but when he saw him next at Whites, he would certainly have it out with the man.

"I suppose you've won the bet and will collect your thousand pounds. I do believe Lord Bankes is here this evening. Maybe he will even give you your winnings and make your day doubly joyful." Lord Carr looked about the room and pointed our Lord Bankes to Henry. "There he is. Shall I go and fetch him for you, Your Grace?"

A cold chill ran down Henry's spine, and he glared at the viscount. "As I said to Lord Bankes, I placed my name in that book well before I knew Miss York, and I asked for my name to be removed. There will be no collection of funds for such a bet."

Lord Carr wagged his finger at Henry as if the fiend had the right to chastise him for anything, even marrying the woman he loved. Who did this little lord think he was?

"Come now, Your Grace. As per the rules of the betting book and as a gentleman, you must collect the blunt. You wagered that you, like many others, would be able to make Miss York fall in love with you, and you succeeded with that gamble. She is now yours. You are married, all contracts are signed. Few would say you did not best us all."

Henry took a calming breath. The man was beyond irritating and too loud for his own good. He did not need Sophie or her friends to hear what he had done. Lord Kemsley had only agreed to keep his secret after discovering he had proposed.

Should Sophie find out, she would be heart-broken and think his affections were only because of some stake. That Kemsley knew of it, too, would be a double blow since she was so close with her cousin and her husband.

Dear God, he needed to keep Carr's mouth shut.

"I will deal with the betting book in good time. Not that it concerns you, Lord Carr. Why do you seem to take so much interest in my wife? And for that matter, why are you here? I did not think you were invited," he said, his temper getting the better of him and causing him to confront the viscount here instead.

"I have known Her Grace for some years. Longer than you, in fact. I think you have forgotten we're old friends. She was a pretty young lady. I remember her well, ripe for the picking. How fortunate you are that you've been the one to pluck her, Your Grace."

Bile rose in his throat, and he fought to tame

his temper. "Perhaps it would be best if you turn your attentions toward your own wife and never speak of the duchess again after this night," he warned.

Lord Carr whistled, his smile grating on Henry's last nerve. "Now, now, Your Grace. There is no need for either of us to get into fisticuffs over a woman whom, had she not had a cousin who married a lofty lord, would still be in the country, possibly a maid at my country estate." Lord Carr threw back his head and laughed. "How amusing is that image? A maid hired to be at my beck and call and do everything that I order her."

Henry fisted his hands at his sides and, catching sight of his wife's concerned glance, fought not to break the viscount's nose.

"But she is not a maid. She is a duchess, and you will never assume such a life for her that is not the one she lives now. Do not denigrate her again, or you shall not like the outcome, my lord."

Carr smirked, lifting his glass of amber liquid in a silent toast. "The duchess should count herself fortunate that her husband thinks so highly of her. She lost my respect many years ago, and I would not hire her now. Gossip in Highclere is very damaging, you understand, and I hear she fled to her cousin's with the help of her mama. Lucky that she did, is it not, since she's now a duchess. Good evening, Your Grace," Lord Carr said, striding away from Henry without a backward glance.

He frowned after his lordship. What gossip was Carr talking of? Sophie was promised a Season with her cousin and nothing more. There was no other reason she left Highclere.

That he knew of ...

TWENTY-ONE

The ball was everything that Sophie hoped it would be. She was a wife, married to a man she loved, and so happy her heart could burst at any moment.

She stood beside Harlow and Lila, their discussion on the *ton* and their plans foremost.

"Our ball is being held soon, but the orchestra I normally use has been reserved by Lady Smale, who decided her rout would be best held on the same evening as our event. I'm much vexed," Lila said, looking at them both for support.

"I have a list of musicians one can hire," Harlow said, sipping her champagne. "I shall send a list around tomorrow with my footman."

Lila threw her sister a small smile. "Thank you, that would be welcome."

Sophie half-listened to her cousin's conversations as the sight of Lord Carr and Henry speaking caught her attention more.

What was Lord Carr doing at their ball at all? She had gone over the final numbers and names only last week with her soon-to-be housekeeper, and she certainly knew that Lord Carr and his wife were not on the list.

But they were here now, and she could not help but feel for his own nefarious reasons.

"What is it about Lord Carr that you dislike so much, Sophie? I have noticed that your disfavor of the man often makes your pretty visage slip."

Sophie turned to Harlow and took a fortifying sip of her champagne. She had never told anyone other than her mama what his lordship had done, and nor would she. No one needed that burden but herself, and she would bear it alone as she had for many years now.

"Lord Carr was very high in the instep and did not associate with many who were not as rich and lofty as he believed himself to be. He's a viscount, I know, but the title is not as old as many in the *ton*, and he often talks down to people. I do not like that about the man nor his wife, who seems to be of similar character."

Lila nodded, glancing in the gentleman's direction. "I have noticed that myself and I have been in town but a moment." She paused.

"So why invite him? Would it not have been

best that they find other entertainments to attend than yours?" Harlow asked, watching Sophie with a directness she was not used to.

"We did not invite either of them, so his being here is an anomaly." She noted her mama gesturing for her from across the room. "If you'll excuse me a moment. Mama is after me. I shall return shortly."

Sophie made her way over to her mama, pausing several times when guests stopped to congratulate her. Their happy tidings soothed a little of her annoyance at Lord Carr being at her wedding ball, but only a very little.

"Darling." Her mama reached for her hand, hers shaking. Sophie studied her parent, watching as the color drained from her visage.

"What is it, Mama? You look as if you've seen a ghost."

"Lord Carr, my dear. He's ..."

Before she could answer and explain his presence, the words she never wanted to be uttered by his mouth murmured behind her.

"Lady Holland, may I congratulate you," Lord Carr said, interrupting what her mother was about to say. "I have not had the opportunity yet to say how wonderful it is that an old friend such as you has married so well."

"You were never friends with my daughter," her mama spat, clasping Sophie's arm as if to save her from a highwayman in the park.

"On the contrary, Mrs. York. We were old friends, as you well know. Friends for some time before I married." He sighed as if remembering happy memories. "I suppose my inability to offer you my hand in marriage turned out to be a welcome reprieve since you're now loftier than most of us in London, and far wealthier."

Sophie flinched and glanced around, hoping no one heard his absurd words. "I never sought your hand in marriage. I never sought anything from you, as you well know. I think it would be best that you leave, my lord."

"I think it would be best that I do not. Not until I tell you what I came here this evening to impart."

"You can say nothing to my daughter that she wishes to hear. Leave," her mother growled, her words brooking no argument.

"No," he quipped, playing with the cufflink pinned to his superfine coat and appearing as a man who looked like nothing in the world bothered him. Not even them telling him to leave. The gall of the man was beyond words.

"As we're old *friends*," he smirked, "I wished to ask now that you're married that I should think you've come into a great sum of money. Or at least you can get your common grubby little hands on it, should you ask."

The pit of Sophie's stomach curdled, and she swallowed, not wishing to cast up her accounts all over the parquetry ballroom floor. "I do not know what funds I have available to me. I have not questioned the Duke of such things."

"That is the optimal word, is it not? Duke. He is one of the richest gentlemen in England. Now, I do not know if you're aware of that, but he is. He has properties in London, Kent, and even a hunting lodge in Skye, Scotland. There is much coin available at your disposal, and I'm going to help you dispose of that capital to your old friend. Me," he said, pointing at his chest.

Sophie frowned, hoping she was not imagining what he was alluding to. He could not possibly! He dare not be such a bastard.

"What is it you want?" Sophie asked when he did not elaborate.

"You will pay me what I want. A lump sum that shall keep my mouth shut in regards to us being lovers all those years ago," he whispered. "What a good jolly time we had, yes?" He tapped her upper arm in a too-familiar way he had no right to.

"Do not dare touch my daughter," her mama growled.

Sophie jerked away from his touch and took a step back. "I will not pay you a farthing, Lord Carr. And we were never what you accuse. That is not how I remember the situation at all."

"Do you not?" He thought upon her words a moment. "But you begged me. You were quite lively if my recollection is correct. Like a spirited filly begging to be broken in, freed of your virtuous bounds."

Sophie closed her eyes, the memories of that night swamping her, threatening to crumble her to her knees. Her head swam, and she felt the reassuring pressure of her mama's clasp upon her arm.

"That is not what happened, and you know that, Lord Carr," she snarled. "How dare you say that was the way of it. You ought to be hung for your actions."

"And yet I shall never be. But I do enjoy replaying them in my mind. You were a wonderful lay."

"You're a bastard," her mother whispered savagely, a word Sophie had never heard her utter. "You are to leave before I make a scene, scandal be damned."

Lord Carr threw back his head and laughed. Several guests smiled over at them, unaware of the threats his lordship was presenting to them.

"There will be no scene because your daughter, Mrs. York will do as I say, or I shall be forced to tell the duke of her conduct when she lived in Highclere. I shall tell the duke how she would come to the great house, my home, and flirt and flutter her eyelashes at me until I gave her what she wanted."

"I was there to give your grandmother company in her ailing days. To read to her and care for her because no one in your family wished to do such a kind thing to an older woman. I never indicated that I wished for you to court me. I blinked like every other woman in the world. I never fluttered anything in your direction, sir."

He smirked and shrugged. "I remember things quite differently, and I shall tell the duke my version of events if you do not do as I wish. I want one thousand pounds before the end of the month. If you can satisfy my fee, then after some consideration, I shall consider whether you're required to pay more for my silence or if I'm satisfied by our trade."

"You're going to blackmail me for the rest of my life? Make me pay for something that was not my doing but yours? And for how long? As long as you deem it necessary? What will ever satisfy you, Lord Carr, for I do not think you ever will be so."

"Well," he drawled. "It is a start, and your funds will keep my wife and me quite well entertained here in London. Unfortunately, money does not go as far as it used to, but with the help of my good friend, the duchess, I shall soon cover my London expenses without delving into my own coffers."

Sophie ground her teeth and ignored his words. "Please escort your wife out of my house,

Lord Carr. Now," she said, not willing to hear a word more from his mouth.

"Of course, Your Grace. I'll look forward to receiving a missive from you in a day or so, but do not delay. Should you not do as I say, I shall not look kindly upon you." He smirked. "I have little doubt that your husband will either. What would he think? Other than you're a charlatan and whore, not the example he wishes for the new Duchess of Holland."

TWENTY-TWO

The following morning Sophie sat in the drawing room with her mama. The housekeeper had set out a lovely breakfast of toast, eggs, ham, and seasonal fruit to enjoy after the successful ball the night before, but she could eat very little. Her stomach still churned at the thought of Lord Carr's threat.

"Where is His Grace this morning?" her mama asked as she picked up her tea and took a satisfying sip.

Sophie did the same and slumped into the cushions of the yellow- and silver-striped silk settee. "He's gone to Whites, but I do not know why. After our ball last evening, I would not think many of our friends would be up this early to venture to their club."

Her mama looked about the room and, satisfied they were alone, met Sophie's gaze. "What are we going to do about Lord Carr, my dear? I think it is best to tell the duke what his lordship did to you and hope that he believes you, not Lord Carr and his disgusting insinuations. If His Grace knows the truth, it voids any trouble Lord Carr can do to you."

"He could always go public with his threats." Sophie's stomach renewed its upset. The idea of anyone other than her mama knowing her secret was too horrific to imagine.

Society would think the poor country mouse had thrown herself at the only lord who lived nearby and had given herself to him in an attempt to secure his hand. Something she had not done and nor ever would. Lord Carr was a toff, a gentleman too high in the instep, and everyone in Highclere knew his disagreeable nature.

But that would also not stop the *ton* from thinking the worst. She was by no means wealthy, and as a way of securing her mama's future happiness and her own well-being in the years to come, many would believe his lordship's lies.

"If he shared his threats, he loses any possibility of receiving payment for his silence. But if the duke knew and protected you with his position in society, Lord Carr would not dare open his mouth. Who would go up against a powerful duke such as Holland? You would indeed be mad if you did."

"He is mad, Mama. You saw him yourself last evening. He's determined to have his money, and

I'm doomed no matter what I decide. Should I pay him for his silence, I know he will return for more. And if I tell Henry what happened to me and what Lord Carr is threatening, I risk ruining my marriage before it has even commenced. Henry may hate me when he learns the truth. He may believe Lord Carr's lies, and then where will I be?"

Her mama's features crumbled, and she regretted her words, but they were the truth. The situation was hopeless. "The duke would not send you away, would he? I can vouch for you for that evening. I can tell him what state you came home in after chaperoning Lord Carr's grandmother at his engagement ball. Your torn dress, bruised face and chest, not to mention other places on your person that were soiled and discolored."

The memory, one she had long tried to forget, to bury well in her past, smothered her yet again, and she took a calming breath, but could not seem to get enough air.

"I cannot breathe, Mama," she said, leaning forward, focusing on the pretty blue-and-white tea set before her as she tried to calm her racing heart.

Her mama came and sat beside her, a comforting hand on her back. "Breathe, dearest. Deep, slow breaths and you will beat this spell." Her mama growled at her side. "Oh, I wish I could eradicate Lord Carr. Be done with the bastard once and for all."

Sophie shook her head, knowing that was not how they would be able to deal with the man. "There is no way I shall be able to ask Henry for a thousand pounds before the end of the month without raising suspicions. I do not even know if the duke has such readily available funds."

"I'm sure he does, dearest, but you are right. He will be curious, and he will unlikely give it to you without knowing why." Her mother's eyes filled with compassion. "You must tell him the truth about your past and hope that he sees reason, believes you, and stands at your side. If he does not, then he is not the man I thought he was."

Sophie nodded, but the idea of telling her account to the man she loved, a man who believed her to be as pure and virginal and unsullied as he was, was too much to bear. Would he judge her cruelly? Would he send her away? Would he shun her and throw her to the wolves, who were the London *ton*?

"I cannot tell Henry. He will be devastated and angry."

"Surely not at you, dearest. He will be furious at Lord Carr, but never you. You did nothing wrong, Sophie. You never did. You did a kindness to his lordship's family, and he attacked you when you walked home. You did not ask for any of his attention."

Her mama pulled her into her arms, and Sophie relented, held tight to her parent, and wished the comforting arms of her mama could sort all her troubles like they did when she was a little girl. But they would not. She had to find a thousand pounds or tell Henry, and unfortunately, a sinking feeling told her it would have to be the latter.

HENRY RODE TO WHITES EARLY, BEFORE most of the gentlemen were present, and went directly to the betting book. He scrolled through the many bets, numerous ones made after the one involving Sophie, and swore.

Where the hell was it?

He flipped through the many pages dating to before the Season had commenced, and still, there was no sign of the page. Working his way through, he looked at the seam of the book and noted that, indeed, a page had been torn from the tome.

He ground his teeth. Who the hell had beaten him at doing such a thing, and why? Henry glanced about the room, not seeing anyone who took an interest in his business with the betting book.

With nothing left to do, he strode over to an empty table and slumped into the leather chair. Someone had the page. Lord Bankes was particularly interested in the bet and had courted Sophie quite adamantly during the Season before her attention diverted to him. Could it be him?

He mulled over the notion a moment before Lord Carr entered the upstairs coffee room and sauntered over to him. A knowing smugness to the man's features was evidence enough of who had stolen the page.

But what could he want with it?

"Your Grace?" Lord Carr said, bowing before sliding into the leather wingback chair across from him. "I was hoping to find you here, although the day after your nuptials, I'm surprised you're here and not in bed with your lovely wife."

Henry's ire grew, and he ground his teeth, reminding himself that violence was not tolerated in Whites and he could not hurt the bastard, no matter how much he wanted to.

"Lord Carr, forgive me for being so forward, but we're not friends, nor shall we be. There is something underhanded about you that I do not like and do not want to associate myself with. I think it is best you leave and socialize with the friends who enjoy your company and cease this longing for us to be acquainted."

"Oh, that does wound." Lord Carr gasped, clasping his chest as if Henry's words had wounded him like a knife to the heart. "But I know we're not friends, and I do not wish to be, but there is something you can do for me so your new marriage remains merry."

"My marriage is not your concern, nor is it on dangerous ground. Leave before I ask for you to be escorted out of Whites."

"I have every right to be here as much as you as a paying member, but I have come here to see you, and I shall say what I must. Now, you may leave, but I would advise you do not, for I think what I have to say will be of interest to you and your future contentment."

Henry did not want to ask him to explain himself, for an unsettling thought in the pit of his stomach told him he already knew what the cur would say. Still, he would not leave until he heard what he wished to impart.

"Very well, what do you wish to explain to me, Lord Carr?" he finally asked, thanking a footman when he delivered two whiskies.

Lord Carr's smile did not reach his eyes, and there was a meanness about this man he did not like. "I have your bet, Your Grace. The one involving the duchess, and you're going to do as I ask, or she'll learn of it. Now, what say you? Are we in business?"

TWENTY-THREE

S everal days later, Sophie strolled through Hyde Park with her mama, her mind far from the picturesque view of the grounds, the water features, the trees, and the numerous horses and carriages that swarmed about the gardens.

The *ton* at play and enjoying the height of the Season appeared as if they did not have a care in the world, and yet she felt as though she were carrying it on her shoulders. It was May, and already she had been married a week. Yet a shadow followed her from when she awoke to when she fell asleep in Henry's arms. A never-ending cycle of doom.

She had three weeks to come up with the thousand pounds, by her calculations. An impossibility that was not achievable, which meant she had only one thing left to do.

She had to tell Henry the truth and hope he would forgive her.

"Have you considered what Lord Carr threatened you with, my dear? I have not wanted to ask as I did not want to add to your stress, but time is ticking by, and I return home to Highclere soon."

Sophie nodded, wishing time could stand still, an impossible dream she knew wasn't logical. "Even if I asked Henry for the money, he would query as to what I needed such an exorbitant amount for, and I would have to come up with an excuse he would not believe," she said, pausing. "No, I will need to tell the truth, but I do not know how to, Mama. What if he becomes enraged? What if he hates me for what has happened?"

Her mama pulled her to a stop and took her hand, squeezing it in support. "He would not dare react in such a way, not when he knows the truth of that day. And I can vouch for you if you wish, speak to him after you have discussed the matter. I can tell him the state you came home in. I think you're worrying about nothing, my dear. His Grace is a good man. He would not treat you so poorly."

"I thought it would be best to tell him soon, today even. He's at home working with his steward this morning, so perhaps when we return to the house?"

"I think that is an excellent idea," her mama said, smiling.

"Your Grace?"

Sophie turned at the feminine voice to find Harlow waving to them atop a nearby carriage, the Duchess of Renford sitting at her side. They made their way over to Harlow and Her Grace, happy to see them both.

"I had hoped to see you here. Are you excited about our ball this evening? Do not forget that everyone is to wear gold," Harlow reminded, excitement thrumming through her voice.

"Good afternoon, Your Grace, Lady Kemsley," Sophie said. "No, I have not forgotten, and the duke and I look forward to this evening." Sophie turned to the duchess, whom she had not seen since her wedding. "How are you, Your Grace? We're so glad you stayed in London for the remainder of the Season. We shall be a jolly bunch at the ball," Sophie said, wishing she could be as happy and carefree as her words suggested.

"As am I. London is always fun this time of year," the Duchess of Renford said, a mischievous light in her eyes.

"I hope you have a gown for this evening, Aunt. The evening would not be complete without you," Harlow stated with a warm smile.

Her mama tittered but shook her head. "Not this evening, my dears. I'm afraid you shall have to weather the ball without me, but I look forward to having tea with you all, and we can catch up on all the gossip then."

"We can certainly arrange that," Sophie agreed.

They bid farewell and started toward their carriage, parked beside a copse of trees that shaded the horses. "I will ask Henry if I can speak to him upon returning home. I will send for you should I need you, Mama."

"All will be well, my dear. Trust in the duke as I do. He will not do you wrong."

Sophie could only hope that was true.

HENRY SHUT THE LEDGER WITH MORE force than necessary and slumped back in his chair. He had been staring at the figures all morning, and no matter how he tried to concentrate on the task at hand, his mind kept wandering to Sophie and what he needed to disclose to her.

She would be hurt, crushed at his disfavor when she learned of the bet. She would assume he courted her to win the thousand pounds. Believe their marriage was not one grown from affection and love but greed and amusement.

All untrue, of course. He loved her more than anything or anyone in his life, but how to prove that fact?

A light knock sounded on his door, and he sat up. "Enter," he called out, relieved to see Sophie peep about the door, her smile warming his soul and taking some of the unease away from his day.

"May I enter?" she asked, keeping to the threshold.

He waved her inside. "Of course, come in. I was just thinking about you," he said. Not an untruth, although not entirely in the way she would consider.

She entered the room and closed the door. He had not seen her since she left their bed this morning, her hair mussed from their many hours of lovemaking the night before, her body free from any garments, including her shift.

His heart gave a pang at how beautiful she was and how fortunate he was to have found her. To have married her. Today she wore a rose-colored morning gown with a short-sleeved spencer and bonnet with matching ribbons.

"You look like springtime personified," he teased.

She untied her hat and set it on the edge of his desk before coming about and sitting on his lap. "I missed you too," she said, wrapping her arms around his neck.

He pulled her close, breathing in her sweet scent that reminded him of jasmine. He stroked her back, her hip, unable to stop touching her. "I have thought of nothing but you all morning. It seems we're truly what one would term newlyweds."

She chuckled, and he reveled in the sound of her happiness. He did not want to admit to the fault that lay in his past. He never wished to hurt her, and the Whites betting book was not what he should have put his name to. In fact, the book should be removed altogether, unfair as it was to the fairer sex, who was usually the target of the men's taunts.

"And is there anything wrong with that?" She closed the space between them and kissed him. He threw himself into the kiss to forget his guilt but for a moment.

She was all soft and womanly curves, everything he adored and could not assuage himself of. A fire lit within him, and he had to have her to remind himself that she was his and nothing would tear them apart, not even a stupid, foolish bet.

He lifted her in his arms, smiled at her faint squeal of surprise, and placed her on his desk. He reached for the hem of her gown, lifting it out of his way to pool at her waist.

Her eyes widened and then darkened with need when she realized his intent. She kissed him hard, her tongue teasing, begging him not to stop. He ripped at his falls, his cock hard and heavy in his hands.

Before he could take her, she reached for him

and stroked him toward madness. His balls tightened, and he reveled in her touch before he could take no more.

"I have to have you," he panted, stepping between her legs. He hoisted her close to the side of the desk, his body craving her, wanting her with a madness that was both frightening and welcome.

She wrapped her legs around his back, her fingers gripped his shoulders, and both moaned when he slipped into her quim. He watched himself take her, slide in and out of her wet notch, his tackle hardening at the erotic vision she made.

Her sob almost undid him, and he thrust into her, taking her with relentless strokes. She kissed him, and it was too much. Her cunny spasmed about his rod, drawing his release forward, and he came hard as her pleasure rippled through her.

He swallowed her scream with a kiss and reveled in the ebb and flow of their orgasms. She rested her head against his chest as they struggled to catch their breaths. "I did not expect such a delightful welcome when I came in here, Your Grace," she teased, using his title.

He slipped free of her, settling her gown back over her knees before tidying up his appearance. His heart raced, and her bedraggled, newly fucked appearance made him want her again.

"I like to please my duchess whenever and however I can."

She slipped from the desk, touching him through his breeches. His cock jumped, and he pressed into her hold. "I'm glad of it, and I look forward to doing this again. Tonight."

As did he, forgetting what he had planned on disclosing to her but minutes before.

TWENTY-FOUR

The Kemsley ball was a crush. Not surprisingly, Henry had lost Sophie some time ago when Lady Kemsley and Lady Billington whisked her away to meet with the Duchess of Blackhaven, who had recently returned from a short trip to Paris.

He wandered through the card room and started for Kemsley, who stood with Viscount Leigh, enjoying a cheroot and whisky. He procured a drink and joined them, taking a cheroot when offered.

"An enjoyable evening," he said to his host and Leigh, who watched the Marquess of Chilsten losing a game of Faro at the table nearby. "Except for Chilsten, perhaps," Kemsley remarked. "I do not think he appears to be enjoying himself at all."

"That's two hundred pounds so far he's lost to Mr. Fairbanks," Leigh disclosed. " I do not think the marchioness will be too pleased when she hears of it."

"If she hears of it," Chilsten quipped, being within earshot. "And if she does, I shall know who to blame," he said without glancing at them.

Henry laughed.

"More funds to keep your mistress happy, Fairbanks," Leigh teased before turning to them and whispering, "I hear he keeps more than one these days and all but a stone's throw from Mayfair."

Henry thought about the gossip. He had not heard such rumors, but then he had been much occupied with Sophie. The thought of her brought a smile to his lips, and he hoped she was enjoying herself.

His pleasant thoughts severed the moment he viewed Lord Carr drawing Sophie to a halt outside the gaming room doors as she passed with Lady Kemsley.

His wife's visage paled, and he was already moving toward them by the time Sophie had wrenched her arm free of the man's hold. Not far from them but held back by several guests who slipped into his way, he waited as patiently as he could to make his way through to help her.

The man would not relent. What was wrong with Lord Carr that he kept singling out Sophie as he did?

The guests in his way moved, and he went to her as quickly as possible.

"You're running out of time to pay me, Your Grace."

The words uttered by Lord Carr stopped him in his tracks. He came to Sophie's side and pushed Lord Carr away, still too close for his liking.

"You will cease accosting my wife, Carr, or there will be an issue between you and me," he warned, not caring that the bastard held the bet he had put his name to in his possession. Even if Sophie found out his stupidity by the wager, that was still better than the gentleman accosting his bride at every ball and party. Did the man fancy an affair with his wife? Did he think he stood a chance at winning her from him?

What a fool if he did.

Lord Carr scoffed. "A problem, Your Grace. You already have an issue with me, and I grow bored of waiting for both of you to do as I want," he said loud enough for others to hear.

Henry stepped close and lowered his voice. "If you have something to say, you may do so in a more private location, but not here," he warned.

Lord Carr raised his brow as if he did not give two figs to what he said or suggested. "I think not, Your Grace. I prefer to do my business here."

Sophie gasped, and her distress reminded Henry of what he had initially heard.

"The library, now, Lord Carr," he warned.

"Maybe we ought to go home, Henry," Sophie suggested, her eyes wide with fear.

Lord Carr's laugh grated on his nerves, and he fought not to lose his temper. "The terrace, Your Grace's. I think the cool air will be required if we're to keep our heads."

Henry took Sophie's hand and led her onto the terrace, not heeding if Lord Carr followed them. The cool night air smelled of soot but was still more refreshing than the stifling, perfumed, and cloying scents of the hundreds of guests inside.

He ensured they were far enough away from those who took the air and steeled himself for what Lord Carr wanted to disclose. He would undoubtedly tell Sophie of his bet, but was there more to his obsession with his wife? Henry's curiosity over their conversation grew.

"What do you want from us, Carr?" He got to the issue. There was no point in easing into this conversation. It was long overdue already.

"Do you wish to know, Your Grace?" he asked, watching Sophie keenly.

"Henry," she said, turning to him. "There is something that I need to explain ..."

"Yes," Lord Carr said, leaning toward them both. "Like how I laid with her before you were married." His lordship leaned against the balustrade, smirking. "Granted, it happened several years ago, but it is still one of my favorite memories of Highclere. Who knew the village girls were so passionate? I did not. Not until that wonderous evening."

Henry stilled, feeling as though the air had been ripped from his lungs. The grounds spun about him, and he stumbled before Sophie helped steady him.

He looked to his wife for an explanation, a denial, but nothing came forth. Her eyes welled with tears, and she clutched his hand. But he could not. Did not want her to touch him. He threw her off and stumbled away from them both, unsure what game they were playing.

"Henry, it is not how Lord Carr is stating. I never ..."

"Was never intimate with him?" he barked, cutting her off. "Were you a virgin when we met? Just answer me that?" he demanded, his life was shattering around him.

She swallowed, her eyes darting to the others on the terrace. "I was not, but Henry ..." She reached for him again, but he could not listen. Not any of her lying excuses. His stomach clenched, and he fought not to cast up his accounts before everyone.

"A shock to you, I see, Your Grace. But it was only one night if that makes it better for you, but your wife is not as sweet and innocent as she led you to believe, and I think you ought to know the truth of these penniless village lasses who come to town to marry well just as she has done. However, there is nothing for it, for you cannot annul your marriage. You've well and truly wedded and bedded her, but you will pay me for my silence if you do not wish for the *ton* to hear what a light-skirt the new Duchess of Holland is." Lord Carr smirked. "Is it not amusing that your father, Your Grace was a great rake, rutted all over London, and died of the pox, and now your very wife is of a similar nature? How you do pick well, Holland. But then, I suppose you cannot choose your parents. A shame, for I certainly would have picked better for myself should I have had the opportunity."

"Henry," he heard Sophie whisper. "This is not how it happened. You know that I'm not like Lord Carr says. Please let me explain." She clasped his arm, and he stared down at her silk-gloved fingers, his mind racing with thoughts. He reached for her and removed her hand with a calmness he did not know he possessed.

"Do not touch me." He did not know what to do or say. How does one react to such news?

"But do not distress, Your Grace," Lord Carr said to Sophie. "The duke is not entirely without fault. You see, you were the butt of a joke at Whites at the beginning of the Season. As pretty and sweet as you were, many who thought you ought to be the diamond, in fact, thought to make a bet about you. Who would win your affection and hand for a thousand pounds? You'll be pleased to know that your husband, Holland won the bet and will collect his blunt. Maybe he'll even give you the funds since you're why he won the money in the first place."

Henry was wrong if he thought Sophie's face couldn't pale any further. She went almost transparent at the disclosure. Her eyes, already filled with tears, turned accusingly toward him.

"Is that true? Did you put your name to a bet about me?" she asked him.

Lord Carr grinned. "Well, Holland, did you or did you not enter your name on a bet?" The bastard Carr fumbled in his coat pocket and pulled out the parchment he had stolen from Whites. "Look for yourself, Duchess. All the proof is here that I speak of."

Sophie reached out and, like a nightmare, unfolded the parchment and read the bet and the numerous names that added to the wager after his own. He heard her exhale, her face crumbling with the realization of what he had done.

"You bastard," Henry said, and before he could stop himself, his fist connected with Lord Carr's nose, and a satisfying crack combined with the gentleman's cry of alarm before he was on top of him, determined to kill the miscreant before the night was finished.

TWENTY-FIVE

Sophie stilled and watched with horror as an anger she had never witnessed enraging Henry took over her husband, and he punched Lord Carr in the nose. The viscount's head snapped back with a force that looked painful even to watch.

But that wasn't enough for her husband. He launched himself and Carr, when he kept his feet, throwing them both onto the balustrade and tumbling into the gardens below.

Gasps from fellow guests sounded, bringing the brawl to the attention of those inside and those taking the air. "Henry, stop," Sophie called, knowing that her husband would not hear her, nor Lord Carr. They tumbled onto the lawn, both men throwing strikes whenever they could.

Lord Carr looked far worse than Henry, as the duke continually flew fists to the man's nose and jaw. For a moment Sophie feared he would kill the viscount before Kemsley and Lord Leigh pushed past her and jumped down to intervene.

For several minutes Lord Kemsley and Lord Leigh fought to pull the men apart, but Henry's punishment against Lord Carr seemed never ending and without remorse.

Sophie started when Harlow took her hand, holding her close to her side as finally, with brute force Henry's friends pulled them apart. The altercation had drawn the attention of everyone at the ball, who seemed to be on the terrace watching with relishing stupefaction.

She wasn't naïve enough not to know that everyone would be talking of them tomorrow. The latest on dit. Every one of them wondering what sparked the argument between the Duke of Holland and Lord Carr.

It would not take them long to remember that Lord Carr came from the same small village of Highclere as did Sophie, and the gossip would spread like an ailment that something was afoot.

Henry climbed the steps, and Sophie watched as the crowd parted for the duke as he moved toward the ballroom. For one horrendous moment, Sophie thought he would continue without her, but he stopped, turned, and gestured her to his side.

She left Harlow and went to Henry, taking his arm and leaving the terrace. He did not speak a word. His arm was tense beneath her palm, his body radiating with anger, his lip bled, and a bruise was already forming on his cheek.

"Henry," she said, beseeching him to listen.

He flinched at her attempt to help him, his gaze steadfast on the ballroom exit. "Not here, Sophie." His voice was stern, as ruthless as his pummeling of Lord Carr, and dread settled in her stomach.

Their carriage ride home was as quiet as death. Sophie watched with trepidation as Henry stared out the window, watching the Mayfair streets with loathing. A muscle worked on his jaw, and she knew he was fighting his anger toward her this time instead of Lord Carr.

When the carriage rolled to a halt before the house, he did not wait for her. Instead, he opened the door and exited, leaving her to follow with the help of a footman who came out to greet them.

By the time Sophie entered the house, Henry was at the top of the stairs, bellowing for his valet. Her maid ran from the back of the house and helped Sophie upstairs. Without many words, as if sensing something was wrong between herself and the duke, her maid helped her change into her shift and nightgown before bidding her goodnight.

Sophie paced her bedroom for several minutes, stopping sporadically and debating entering Henry's room. Masculine voices too soft to be understood sounded next door, and water splashed. Was Henry washing his wounds? She needed to help him and care for him.

Unsure of what she should do, Sophie went to her sideboard and poured herself a glass of claret, downing it quickly before pouring another. Was he going to come to speak to her or ignore her for the rest of the night?

What was he thinking?

She chewed her nails as she paced her bedroom floor. He would be angry and hurt, but then she also had a good reason to be. He had included himself on a bet that was about her. Granted, it was perhaps made before he knew her, and the bet wasn't as bad as she had done. But then, what Lord Carr had insinuated and what Henry believed was not true either.

She heard further commands, and then the snick of the lock on their connecting door put paid to her entering through that door. Sophie stood, staring at the entry for several minutes, wondering if she had truly heard herself being locked out of Henry's room.

Unable to believe it, she strode to the door and tried the handle. It did not budge. "Henry, let me in. We need to talk," she yelled at the wood. No answer sounded and before she could think twice, she strode from the room and down the passage to Henry's suite.

She tried that door, but it, too, was locked.

"Henry!" she wailed, banging on the dark wood. "Do not lock me out, please," she begged.

"Your Grace, the duke is not to be disturbed this evening. It would be best if you retired for the evening," Henry's valet said from the servant's stairs behind her.

Without answering him, her pride taking hold, she kicked the door with her slippered foot and then, without another word, went back to her room, slamming the door in the servant's face.

How dare Henry lock her out in such a way. How could he not want to hear her side of the story? She threw herself on her bed, fighting the tears that threatened her. She would speak to him first thing in the morning, make him listen to her. Her mama knew the truth of that long-ago nightmare in Highclere. Henry would have to believe her mama. He would not think badly of her parent too. Even if he believed Sophie to be a charlatan of the worst kind.

***

HENRY WOKE EARLY THE FOLLOWING morning and made his way down to the library. He locked the door and worked on numerous ledgers, unpaid bills that mounted over the last week, and several missives from his tenants and estate managers both in Kent and Scotland.

Sophie had tried three times last evening to speak to him, and he had ignored her imploring. The sound of her sweet voice almost crumbled his resolve not to see her, but he could not tumble so easily.

She had not been a maid?

She had given herself to Lord Carr?

He picked up his glass of brandy and launched it across the room, narrowing his eyes and grounding his teeth as the glass splintered into a million pieces.

Shaking his head, he rubbed a hand over his jaw, unable to get the image out of his head of the woman he loved in the throes of passion in Carr's arms. He should have killed the bastard last night. How dare he even breathe near his duchess?

The many weeks of his interest in Sophie became clear. He had her once, and he was determined to have her again, and when it became obvious that he would not, he tried to bribe his wife in exchange for his silence.

Undoubtedly, the yellow, bottle-headed fool was already assisting the rumor mill over what occurred last evening. Ruining Sophie's reputation with delight.

Their Season was over. A lot of the reason as to why his fault. He should not have hit Carr, but knowing that man had been with his wife, Henry's reaction was swift and punishing. Before he could think clearly, he had Carr on the lawn and could not stop punching the ugly bastard's face.

He was unsure what would have happened had Kemsley and Leigh not stepped in and stopped him.

"Henry, please speak to me," he heard Sophie's muffled voice call from behind the library door.

He tapped his quill against the desk. He could not stay here. If he stayed, they would only argue further, which would not do them any favors. He still had his rooms at the Albany. He would go there, take his valet and remove himself from the household and think upon what he would do, how he would react, and move forward with what he now knew.

But he did have to confront Sophie, now better than any other time. He stood and strode to the door, unlocking it. The image of her before him, her sickly features, as if she had slept as little as he, pleaded for him to forgive her. But he could not.

She has been intimate with Lord Carr. Do not fall for her soft features that beg for forgiveness.

He pushed past her, moving toward the stairs. "I'm leaving. You may remain here until I have decided what to do with this information that came to light at last evening's ball."

"Henry, please, do not go. We need to talk. You must know the truth, please," she begged him, clasping his arm in an attempt to stop him. He removed himself from her grasp and did not stop. "When I have decided, I shall be back. I do not want to hear anything from you right now. Nothing at all," he barked, not meeting her eye.

He swallowed hard when she stopped at the bottom of the stairs, and he could feel her watching him, feel her despair as thick as his own.

Do not relent. Do not look back.

He would not be weak, not when he needed to be strong, for himself and the dukedom. That was most important right now, not his duchess, who had fucked another and then lied about the fact.

TWENTY-SIX

Henry had been absent from their home for several days, and each day Sophie woke with the hope that he would return. That he would seek her out and finally hear her side of the account.

Each day she retired, disappointed and heart sore. Crying oneself to sleep was never ideal, and she was at a loss as to what to do. Her mama's time in London would soon cease, as she was leaving for Highclere tomorrow. Sophie debated going with her, leaving this town that had thrown her to the wolves, her husband included in those villains.

She could only remember one other time when she had felt so alone and lost. That the man she loved had placed her again into the shady place was unforgivable.

Why would he not listen to her?

"Sophie?" Harlow's soothing voice sounded

at the door of her private parlor, and she turned to see her cousin entering the room and shutting the door firmly behind her. "Why have you not allowed me to call? I've come every day and been turned away."

"How did you get in?" she asked, ashamed that she had not wanted to see her family, other than her mama.

"I pushed past the footman and threatened him when he attempted to stop me."

The image brought a small smile to Sophie's lips, and she shuffled over on the settee when Harlow sat beside her. "What has happened? Rumors are flying all over London that the duke has left you, and you are having an illicit affair with Lord Carr?"

Sophie sighed, the thought of such a horror raising bile in her throat. "The truth is much less titillating than that. It is not pleasant. Are you sure you wish to hear it?" she asked, knowing what Harlow would learn would not be easy.

"Please tell me what happened. Lord Carr is walking around London with a blackened face, and Henry is locked up in his rooms at the Albany. Kemsley made some inquiries and found out where he was staying."

So that was where Henry had gone. At least she knew now, that was something. She had feared he had returned to his country estate in Kent. Sophie took a deep breath, met Harlow's eyes, and told her everything that had happened in Highclere, not leaving one detail out of what transpired during the rape.

When she had finished, Harlow fumbled for her handkerchief and dabbed at her cheeks, but Sophie could no longer cry. She had spilled enough tears for her lost innocence many years ago. Her hope of a happy ever after with Henry seemed destined to be ripped from her, too, thanks to Lord Carr. A future that Henry had allowed to be stolen.

"Sophie ..." Harlow whispered, pulling her into her arms and squeezing her so hard that Sophie thought she might swoon. She patted her cousin's back, comforting her in an odd turn of events.

"I do not know what to say other than I'm so sorry, my darling friend. I wish I could change what happened to you."

Sophie pulled back and threw her a small smile. "There is nothing anyone can do, and I resolved myself long ago to try to forget that night and hope for a better future, which I thought I succeeded with. You offered me a Season, such a privilege, and I'm so thankful you were so kind to a poor relation, and then I met Henry, and my limited circumstances did not seem to worry him. But Lord Carr made Henry think that what happened in Highclere was desired by both of us. I do not think he believes or trusts me. He will not even listen to what I have to say. Just left me here alone."

"Well," Harlow huffed, her mouth twisting into a displeased line. "Holland needs a good kick in the backside for not giving you a chance to explain, at least. What are you going to do?"

"I thought I may return to Highclere with Mama. I do not think my marriage is a union that can work anymore. Henry's departure and cold silence prove his disgust for me. I think it is best that I leave and do everyone a blessing and never return." Sophie paused, thinking of Henry's bet.

"Holland loves you, Sophie, you must trust in what you feel for each other and not allow anything to come between you."

"There is the possibility that Holland only courted me in the first place because of a bet at Whites." Harlow threw her a confused frown and Sophie continued, "I was a wager from all accounts. One thousand pounds for anyone who was able to make me fall in love with them. How fortunate that my husband won the bet."

Harlow gasped, her face paling. "Tell me that is not true."

Sophie sighed, wishing it were not but unable to ease her cousin's shock. "It is true I'm afraid, and a truth Lord Carr gleefully informed me of. It is why I think my marriage may be doomed. I do not really know for sure if Henry desired me enough to court me in the first place, or that he merely wished to see if he could win the money."

"No," Harlow growled. "I do not believe so ill of Holland and you will not travel to Highclere as if you've done something wrong, for you have not. Lord Carr should be the one run out of town, not you. As for the duke, he will not get away with this silence or this scandalous bet you speak of. I shall ensure that he does not continue hiding and not facing this truth. He is your husband and needs to listen to you, needs to make amends for this vulgar wager."

Sophie wished that were true, but she did not think such a prospect was feasible. After so many days of wallowing in pity, it was hard to be optimistic.

"What do you suggest I do?" Sophie asked.

"You will attend the Fox ball this evening as if Holland and Lord Carr's fisticuffs were nothing of consequence. No one knows the truth of what you say, Lord Carr is certainly not spreading such rumors, but he's also not denying the affair, which we need to heed and stop posthaste. By facing him, giving the cut direct will help people realize nothing ever was between you. And society, thankfully, will support a duchess before a viscount. We can win that part of the war, at least. As for Holland, you shall have to fight His Grace at another time."

Sophie nodded, understanding what Harlow

was saying and wondering if she had the strength to face society. To rise above the rumors, laugh at their silly tales, and fight for her position that she had gained through love, not scandal or trickery as many believed.

"You cannot leave," Harlow said again. "To do so would make you appear guilty of what they're saying about you."

Sophie stood and rang for a servant. A footman appeared momentarily at the parlor door. "Please check to see if I have been invited to the Fox ball this evening, Geoffrey, and if I have, please send a note to Lady Fox that I will be in attendance."

"Yes, Your Grace. I shall inform you presently."

Sophie turned to Harlow, who appeared pleased for the first time that day. She, too, felt a little lighter in the soul, as if she were being proactive in fighting Carr instead of the opposite.

"Good, now let us go upstairs and find the most regal dress you possess. Tonight the *ton* will see the Duchess of Holland. See that she is not shamed or cowed by Lord Carr and his lies. Tonight you will own society, just as is your right, and I shall be beside you the whole time."

HENRY STARED OUT AT THE COURTYARD of the Albany and downed another glass of whisky. Piccadilly Road blurred before him, and he blinked several times before it became clearer.

He had left Sophie a week ago today, and still, the anger that thrummed through him had not dissipated. Although he could not say what offended him more, his running away from his wife or what Lord Carr had implied.

Something told him it was both in equal measure.

Shame washed through him. He had done her wrong by not listening to what she had to say or explaining the wager Carr spoke of. He could have at least afforded her that if nothing else. He closed his eyes, recalling the moment Sophie learned of the betting book and her involvement in it. Her face had paled, and he had seen the pain in her eyes. A pain that he had caused. So many wrongs between them, however were they to move forward together? That he could not answer and with the Season almost at an end, time was running out to do so.

Mayhap he could flee to Scotland. Hide away in the highlands during the winter and only return when he had controlled his temper.

He ground his teeth, knowing that should he see Lord Carr, he would call him out. The memory of besting the little beast brought a smile to his lips. He had enjoyed hearing the man's teeth crack more than he thought he would. That the bastard dared lay a hand on his wife made his blood chill to ice in his veins.

He ran a hand through his hair. What a mug he was. That he had professed his abstinence and marveled that they had given each other the sweetest gift made him shudder in disgust. How she must have laughed at him and his gullible nature.

That she was well-versed in the act of sex, the thought of all they did before marriage made sense now. Explained how very talented and reactive she had been in his arms.

She knew the nature of men and had done things to him no maid would ever have attempted. Was that because she had done those sexual things to Lord Carr?

"Fucking bastard," he bellowed, punching the wall beside the window. The cut on his hand, not yet healed from one of Lord Carr's teeth, opened and dripped blood on the floor.

He stared at it momentarily and ignored the renewed pain before walking to the whisky decanter and pouring another sizeable glass. Downing the drink, he poured another, slumping into a chair, only content when darkness overtook his vision and peace claimed him.

TWENTY-SEVEN

S ophie wore an opaque purple gown that, under candlelight, shimmered and appeared almost black. If the *ton* wanted a woman who had fallen from grace, she would dress to suit the part and have them say such things to her face.

Not that she thought the *ton* would be so bold as to do so. She trusted what Harlow had said. The *ton*, for all their viperish ways, would not cut a duchess, not without absolute proof, which there was none.

And rightfully so, since she had never been with Lord Carr in the way they imagined. Just the thought of an affair with Carr made her shiver in revulsion, and she would not let him win a second time.

He would not force her out of London when she had done nothing wrong. He was the individual who should be ashamed and leave.

She would not.

Sophie raised her chin and thanked Lord Kemsley as he helped her from the carriage. Linking arms with Harlow, they walked into Lord and Lady Fox's Georgian mansion and started toward the ballroom doors.

The house was brimming with guests milling everywhere, the ballroom a crush and dancing already underway. A minuet played as they moved into the room, looking out for those closest to them. Tonight Sophie had worn the ducal jewels, demanding that those who did not recall and needed a reminder that she was the Duchess of Holland and would not cower at home, ashamed of an untrue on dit.

Lord and Lady Fox came and greeted them. Lady Fox was exceedingly gracious to Sophie and settled some of her nerves at being there. With her ladyship's generous welcome, it soon brought forth an array of guests to greet them, and it was only minutes until they were ensconced in a group of guests talking of the ball and the Season in general.

Sophie made a point of including herself in the conversation as much as possible. Her goal this evening was to appear nonchalant, even if many had not missed that Holland was not with her.

Nor could she see him in attendance herself. Was he still closeted away in his rooms at the Albany? She ought to call on him, demand that he speak to her, and make him apologize for not listening to her.

She deserved to be heard, at the very least. After all Henry professed to feel for her, his love and adoration sounded hollow when he would not even hear her side.

Anger burned hotter within her, turning to searing fury when Lord Carr dared to join their group with his wife. Sophie looked to Harlow, who pulled her to walk away. They only managed a few steps when the grating sound of Lord Carr's voice sounded behind them.

"Your Grace, Lady Kemsley, how striking you both look this evening. I was just telling my dear wife, Lady Carr, that we should come to speak to you."

Sophie turned and did not miss the knowing smirk that sat on Lady Carr's cool visage. How well her ladyship suited Lord Carr. Mean, cruel-spirited pair who ought not be speaking to her at all.

Sophie turned, not the least interested in anything either of them had to say.

"I do not think there is much to be said between us, my lord," Harlow cut in before Sophie could utter a word. "We are not friends, which may or may not surprise you, but one fact you ought to heed."

"Oh, come now," Lady Carr tittered. "You as

well as I know the rumors between our families are untrue. There is no reason for us not to be friends."

"But your husband blackmailing the duke and myself is not a reason, or have you not told Lady Carr of your underhanded ways, my lord?" Sophie asked, wondering if he would own to his misdeeds.

Lady Carr waved Sophie's words aside. "He did not mean anything by those threats. We do not need your money, Your Grace."

"Indeed," Lord Carr agreed. "It was a mere game, you understand. A tournament I like to play when I know things about someone. If anything, you ought to be thanking me. For if it were not for myself, you would never have known of the bet at Whites that involved you. I do hope I have not caused trouble between yourself and the duke."

His lordship's merriment grated on Sophie's nerves, and she studied him a moment, his lip still healing from Henry's fist splitting it open. "I do not associate with liars, and you've done nothing but cause trouble for me here in London. You threw what you believed to be true in your own warped mind against the duke, knowing it would cause strife. You are a liar, sir. You are reprehensible."

Lord Carr's eyes narrowed at her words, and he stepped close. "Let us not quarrel, Your Grace.

I would hate for our truth to be heard in the middle of a ball. We need to pretend to be friends and acquaintances with no hard feelings between us all if we're to survive the Season."

"I do not need you to survive the Season. I'm the Duchess of Holland, but know this," she said, bending toward his side. "I will ruin your wife's chances to move forward and prosper in society should you not stem these rumors of us. You forced me all those years ago, raped me, and you know you did. If you want your children and their children's children to have great marriages and keep your minuscule estate prosperous, you will do as I say, and from this night, never darken another ball that I'm to attend ever again. Do you understand, *my lord*?"

He glanced about nervously. "Of course, Your Grace. I understand perfectly. No harm meant, truly. I only wished to recount old times."

"Of course you did, dearest," Lady Carr said, patting his arm.

Sophie nodded toward the ballroom door. "I believe you have another event to attend this evening, so we would hate to keep you a moment longer. Good evening to you both," Sophie said, forcing the nerves down that threatened her knees and made her voice tremble.

How she loathed Carr. Being so close to him made her want to run, yet she could not. No longer would she allow him to make her cower and hide from the past. Hide from him.

He was the hazard, not her. He was the villain, she the victim, and no longer would she allow him to have any power over her.

"But we've only just arrived," Lady Carr argued, looking to her husband for clarification.

Lord Carr schooled his features and made a solid attempt to appear agreeable to Sophie's command. But his eyes, a window to a person's soul, were cold and alight with annoyance at her threat.

"The Mason's ball, my dear. We have such a busy schedule that we're all over Mayfair this evening. Thank you for reminding me, Your Grace." He threw her a small smile. "Good evening to you both."

"Goodbye," Sophie stated, the last word she would ever utter to the man. Harlow did not bother to say her goodbyes at all.

They watched in satisfaction as the Carrs left the ball. With his leaving, a weight lifted from Sophie's shoulders for the first time in days. She had defended herself and her husband. Never again would she allow Carr any power over her, not in society or her own mind.

"I'm so proud of you, Sophie," Harlow said, squeezing her arm and moving them toward a footman holding a silver salver of champagne.

They procured a glass each and tapped the edge of the crystal flutes together in salute.

"Here's to your future and for making Lord Carr run away like a scared little boy."

Sophie laughed for the first time since Henry had left, and the future seemed much brighter, more possible. All that was required now was for Henry to apologize for the wager he had yet to explain and to give her what she deserved, a moment of his time.

He would believe her, the stubborn fool, and if he did, maybe she would think about listening to why he'd included his name in the Whites betting book. "I'll not be looked down on by anyone in this society for crimes that were not mine. Henry will come around, and if he does not, then that will be his mistake," she said, hoping it did not come to that but unwilling to bend for anyone again. Not when it came to her sanity and health.

Harlow tapped her glass a second time against hers. "That deserves another toast."

And so it did.

TWENTY-EIGHT

D ays passed, and Henry lost himself in a game of oblivion and disorientation. For several minutes, he had sat at his desk in his lodgings, fighting to remember the day and when he had bathed last.

He lifted his arm and sniffed himself. The stench hit him with a force that made him recoil, and he leaned back in his chair, disgusted at his actions this past week. Or was it two now? He could not remember.

Voices sounded in the small foyer of his rooms, and before he could ask his valet who it was, the door slammed open, and Lord Kemsley stood glaring at him from the threshold.

Henry raised his brow, staring back. His friend's presence did not bode well for him since he had sought him out. And gathering from his irate visage, Kemsley's visit was not a sociable call.

"Ah, so here you are," Kemsley said, striding

into the room and slamming the door with as much force as he had opened it. "I see you've made yourself quite at home in your rooms here," he said, going over to a window and hoisting up the pane of glass. Cool, afternoon air entered, and Henry scowled.

"Would you care for a drink?" Henry offered, going to the whisky decanter and pouring himself one. Kemsley stood, fisting his hands on his hips.

"No, and I think you've had plenty of the amber liquid to last you a lifetime." Kemsley gestured toward him. "Have you seen yourself, man? You have not shaved in a week at least, and as for the smell permeating this room, well, I would think you've not bathed in a year."

Henry shrugged, supposing that was probably true, not that he cared. He did not care for anything anymore. His wife, the woman he loved, had been intimate with another. She had given herself to a man that was not him. Did she care for Lord Carr? Love him?

The thought made him choke on his drink.

"There is no one here to care about such facts," Henry retorted. "And when you leave, you too will cease to smell my stench. Feel free to excuse yourself whenever you wish, my lord," he slurred, slumping back into his chair.

Kemsley's face mottled in a temper, and Henry raised his hand, shaking one finger at the earl. "Now, now, Kemsley. After my run-in with Carr, my nose has only just healed, along with my lip. I do not need you bloodying up my features yet again."

"You deserve a good thumping after your actions these past weeks." Kemsley strode to the desk, towering over him while he sat. "Do you have any idea what damage, possibly irreversible harm, you're making while sitting here on your ass, wallowing in your delusions regarding the duchess?"

He flinched at the mention of Sophie, but nor did he like him having an opinion and voicing it to his face. What did it have to do with Kemsley? He knew nothing of what Sophie had told him. He did not know the truth about his wife's actions. Had Kemsley known, he may have thought twice about allowing her into his home and sponsoring her for the Season.

"They are not delusions. I know full well what I'm doing and you would react the same should you know what I do about Miss York."

"Miss York?" Kemsley stuttered, staring at him as if he had lost control of his senses. In truth, he may have, especially when it came to his wife.

"You would not insult her by calling her such a name. She is married to you. The Duchess of Holland forevermore. No blasted rumor or needling by Lord Carr will change that fact. You need to go see Her Grace and beg for forgiveness before it is too late."

Too late? Too late for what? The pit of his stomach twisted, and he wondered if Kemsley knew something he did not. But as to what he could not say and in his spinning haze, he did not care. She had misled him. Lain with another before their marriage. The idea made him want to vomit.

"There is little to be said between us. The duchess," he said, smirking for good measure at Kemsley, "is a liar, and I do not wish to see her," he lied, knowing he longed to see her, touch her, be with her every aching moment of his life. He was not so wholly innocent in their estrangement. He too had played a part in tearing them from each other, one that Carr used to his advantage. Not that he would admit to such weaknesses to Kemsley.

"You made a promise to my wife's cousin. You will not break her heart and the vows said before God, Holland, or you will end up with another bloody nose."

Henry had heard enough. He pushed back his chair, slamming it against the bookcase at his back. "And who are you to criticize me? I'm the Duke of Holland, one of the highest-ranking gentlemen in London. And gentlemen being the optimal word. Who are you, Lord Kemsley? Well," he scoffed. "Let me tell you who you are.

You are an earl who taught a woman, a maid, who was not your wife, how to seduce other men while sampling those goods yourself. How dare you come into my home and criticize me for re-acting to the news of my wife's disgrace with something resembling acceptance and non-chalance."

"You will never again speak of Lady Kemsley with anything other than respect ever again, I warn you. While I grant I was not always the up-standing gentleman, I did marry the countess without scandal ever kissing her name. But the same cannot be said for you. You fought with an-other man before the whole *ton* and then moved out of your home. You left your wife to face the *ton* alone to try to salvage what is left of both your reputations and the Holland name."

Henry ran a hand through his hair and strode across the room. He glanced up at a painting of his father, the blaggard that he was, and hated everything about everyone.

"The fight with Carr was nothing, and no one needed to read into it other than two men who did not like one another. Nothing more."

"Except Carr helped spread the rumor that your wife was having an affair with him, and you became aware of the fact."

"That was not what happened." The truth was far worse than that. He cringed. "Did you know that Sophie gave herself to him some years before her Season? In Highclere, before she met me," he blurted, voicing the horrific details of her secret for the first time to another. Not that it helped to say the words aloud. They still sounded as harrowing as the first time he listened to them. "She made love to him. Was she in love with him?" He shook his head. "That I do not know. I did not stay around to find out."

"You're a bloody fool." Kemsley hoisted him by the cuff of his shirt and threw him up against a wall, the painting of his father tipping awkwardly to one side. "Made love? To Carr! Have you spoken to the duchess? Have you given her the right, the respect to hear what she has to say about all of this sorry tale, or have you only allowed Carr to voice his side?" Kemsley asked him.

Henry swallowed, pushing Kemsley away and stumbling to the side. "What, it was not making love for the duchess? Are you telling me that she fucked him instead?"

A fist connected with his nose a second time in as many weeks, and his head snapped back against the wall. He slid to the floor and did not get up, not in the mood to take another beating, and certainly not from one of his friends. Or who was once his friend?

"Go to the duchess and beg her for forgiveness because you're living in a fool's nightmare at this very moment. You do not know the truth of the matter at all, and I won't be the one to burst the righteous cocoon you've made for yourself here. You're being a prig, and if you do not make this right, I will be back, and you'll receive more than a bloody nose."

Henry stumbled to his feet, coming eye to eye with Kemsley. "Do not forget who I am, Kemsley," he warned. How dare Kemsley threaten him? But a little part of his mind seized at what Kemsley knew that he did not.

"It's not a warning, *Your Grace*," he spat with sarcasm. "It is a promise. You will go to the duchess tomorrow evening after you have sobered up and hear her truth. Then and only then will I call you a friend once more."

Henry scoffed, striding away. "I have other friends, Kemsley. And when I'm ready, I shall speak to my wife and hear her truth. Little good it will do her. She has admitted to the night of passion, I do not wish to know any more than I already do."

Kemsley shook his head, moving toward the door with determined strides. "You do need to hear more and I'll be back if you do not make this right."

Henry watched him leave, marveling at his mettle but thinking upon it too. He had a choice to make, and if he did as Kemsley said, he needed to be sober when he made it.

TWENTY-NINE

Henry did not know of what ball he was in attendance. The room blurred into insignificance the moment he spied Sophie across the ballroom floor. This evening she wore a ruby empire-cut gown with a bodice that left little to a man's imagination. The dress had hundreds of tiny sparking jewels sewn upon it, and they glistened with her every move or flicker of candlelight.

His duchess caught the attention of anyone present.

His especially.

He watched her without her awareness. She was beautiful and joyful as she stood with a group of ladies, deep in conversation and enjoying the ball. After Kemsley's visit, he thought about his actions and reactions to what he had learned about Sophie and Lord Carr.

Guilt prickled and warned him that his response was not what it should have been. At the very least, he should have given her the opportunity to explain what had happened. Lord Carr had never been a particularly truthful gentleman. He should not have believed his anecdote so quickly and ignored his wife's pleas after the fact.

What a bastard he had been.

He waved away the opportunity for wine from a passing footman. His consumption of such liquid was too excessive of late, and he wanted a clear, cool head this evening. Sophie deserved no less.

That is if she would speak to him.

She would be well within her bounds to refuse to.

The thought that he had made a mistake in judging her, punishing her without giving her the time to explain, was ungentlemanly and contemptible. Even his reason as to why he reacted in such a way was no excuse.

He loved her.

Adored her more than was possibly healthy.

The idea that she had given herself to another broke him in two. After hearing of her past, he had concluded that Sophie giving herself to Carr had been a mutual decision.

But after Kemsley's visit the other evening, he was no longer so sure. His friend had hinted that there was more to that night that involved Sophie that he needed to hear and know.

The thought that her secret was not of her making made his blood run cold.

She laughed, her eyes sparkling in amusement, and his chest hurt that he was not beside her, being part of what made her merry. For the past two weeks, he had been nothing but misery in her life.

He ought to be horsewhipped.

The idea, too horrendous to imagine, floated through his mind yet again. What if Sophie did not permit her night with Lord Carr? A rage unlike any he'd ever sensed flickered to life at the thought. What if he had judged her, thrown her aside, his wife, his heart and love, and because of a lie?

Sophie glanced up, and their eyes met, held. She studied him momentarily before her lips thinned into a displeased line, and she moved her attention elsewhere.

Dear God, she hated him.

He had lost her because he was a stupid, pigheaded fool who would not listen.

"She will speak to you if you ask her to," Kemsley said, coming up to his side and throwing him a resigned look.

Henry clamped his jaw shut and fought the emotion that coiled within him. He had made a mistake. No matter what Sophie needed to tell him, he knew he could not turn his back on her.

He could not hate her whether she went to Lord Carr's bed willingly or against her will.

He loved her no matter what, and seeing her again only cemented that fact.

"Will she?" he said, not taking his eyes off his wife.

"She will, and you will listen to her, and you will right whatever wrongs between you because you love her as she loves you. You will make this right, Holland. I have faith in you, my friend," he said, clapping him on the back before moving off into the crowd.

He watched as Sophie was asked to dance by Mr. Temple and led out onto the ballroom floor. Jealousy coursed through his blood as he watched her be spun about the room, enjoying her evening, and not in the arms of her husband.

He deserved to watch her with another after treating her so disrespectfully, ignoring her pleas for him to listen. He deserved everything she meted out.

He did not deserve her love. That was more than evident tonight.

SOPHIE DID HER VERY BEST TO IGNORE Henry, who stood in the ballroom watching her every move. She ignored the pit of her stomach that churned at the despondent countenance that settled on his person.

She would not forgive him. Not after his weeks of silence and abandonment. He deserved to rot in his pool of loathing for her, stay there, and never leave.

Mr. Temple said something, and she nodded, agreeing without having to participate too much in their conversation while they danced. Not that she could concentrate, not with her handsome husband watching her every move. She could feel his eyes burning a path up her spine whenever she gave him her back.

She supposed she was a little put-off, taken aback that he was here at all. He had not reached out to her since the day he had stormed from their home two weeks before.

Did his presence here this evening mean he was willing to listen to her? Little good that would do him now. He had his chance to hear what the woman he was supposed to love had to say, and he had ignored her pleas.

Instead, he had believed that cur Lord Carr and left her alone in their home.

Well, not entirely alone, she supposed. Her stomach flipped at the hope that she was carrying their child. At first, she thought her sickness and upset stomach had been due to Henry's leaving, but as the days passed and the sickness became more regular and severe, she was not so sure.

Of course, she was still upset that Henry refused to listen to her, but anger had replaced those emotions. But the sickness prevailed.

Her maid, indeed, had noted her condition and had started to bring in ginger biscuits each morning along with her cup of tea.

She supposed she would have to tell Henry her news, not that he deserved to know. Shame washed through her. No, he would be pleased he was to be a father. That was if he believed the child was his and not someone else's.

Who knew what was going through that man's mind after so many days of being locked up in his lodgings?

The dance came to an end, and instead of leading her back to her group of friends, Mr. Temple walked her toward Henry. Panic assailed her at having to speak to Henry. The idea of fleeing back to her friends almost made her take the first step, but no. She needed to face him and whatever future they would have. If they had one.

"Your Grace," Mr. Temple said, placing Sophie's hand on Henry's arm as if she were being given away like a sacrificial lamb. "Good evening to you both," he said before leaving them.

Sophie could feel the eyes of the *ton* sporadically looking their way. She kept her gaze ahead of her on the dancing couples, knowing that if she looked at Henry, her defenses might crumble.

And they could not. He needed to know he could not treat her so abhorrently ever again.

"Sophie?"

Her whispered name made her want to throw herself into his arms. Beg him to listen, to understand. "Your Grace, I did not expect to see you here this evening," she replied, glad her voice remained emotionless. A good start and one she needed to continue.

"I wanted to see you." He reached for her hand, clasping it in his. His thumb rubbed the top of hers in a comforting embrace he often did. Little good it would do him.

"Really?" she said, attempting to sound shocked. She met his gaze and raised her brows. "After two weeks of silence, I find that hard to believe. You are not here to see me, Your Grace. You're here to see who else I can throw myself at, so you may also judge me on that."

"Never," he sighed. "Let us return home and speak. I'm ready to listen now. I was not before, and I apologize for that."

"Oh, you're ready," she scoffed. "And you're sorry." She shook her head, her temper taking hold. She wanted to hurt him, be cruel, cold and unkind, just as he had been. Against her nature and better judgment, she could not stop. Sophie pulled her hand free, ignoring the pleading light in his eyes.

"I'm here to enjoy the ball. If you're home

when I return, we may then speak but do not expect me to be home early. I shall return when I'm ready. Good evening, Your Grace," she said, leaving him gaping after her.

Sophie strode away, using all the willpower she could to do so.

Nothing had ever been so hard in her life.

THIRTY

S ophie arrived home late and stumbled to a stop in the foyer at the sight of Henry waiting for her at the threshold of the library door.

"What are you doing here?" she asked, moving toward the staircase, in no mood to speak to him, not after how he had treated her. "Should you not be at your rooms at the Albany?" she spat, not attempting to hide the sneer in her voice. What did he expect? A sweet homecoming?

"We need to talk, Sophie. I know I should have heard what you had to say, and I'm sorry I did not. Please," he begged, moving toward her. "Please tell me what happened with Lord Carr. I shall not judge, I promise you. I just want to know the truth. From you."

She scoffed, wondering what had brought on this change of heart this night. He had certainly not wanted to hear anything from her before. She thought on it a moment before conceding.

"Very well, I shall tell you everything, but know this, Holland," she said, using his title and not his given name. "No matter what you think or feel over the situation, it cannot be changed, and I will no longer feel as if I were in the wrong or had done something bad to cause what happened to me. Do you understand what I'm saying to you?" Needing him to comprehend that she would not relent. Lord Carr was at fault in every way, and she would not be looked down upon because of a man's actions and choices.

"I understand," he agreed.

Sophie followed him into the library and shut the door, locking it against interruptions. Her hands shook, and she clasped them at her front, steeling herself to tell him what he needed to know.

The memory was not kind, and her knees threatened to give way at the recollection.

"What did Lord Carr do, Sophie?" he asked, a small frown between his brows.

Sophie settled in the chair across from Henry and organized her thoughts. She would tell him everything as it happened and hope he would not judge. Should he do so, she knew what that would mean for them both. The end of their marriage. Henry's reaction tonight would determine their future.

"Sophie?" he questioned further when she did not say a word.

She cleared her thoughts and took a deep breath.

All would be well. He would not hate her. Surely he would not.

"There are some things that happened to me while I lived at Highclere that I have not told you. Until recently, I had not told anyone other than my mama."

"Who does know what you speak of?" he asked, studying her as if she were an oddity he had not seen before. And perhaps she would be after he learned the truth.

"Mama and now Lady Kemsley know the truth," she said, and the blaggard Lord Carr, but she did not voice that.

"Very well," he said, the hurt in his tone clear to hear.

Angry as she was at Henry, Sophie hated that he had found out by someone else and not from her. He deserved to know whom he was marrying and what baggage she carried. "I will tell you everything but do not say anything or react until I have finished," she said, meeting his gaze. "Promise me that you will agree."

He nodded, a muscle working in his jaw. "I promise, now tell me of that night?"

She remembered her time in Highclere, one she had adored, a life full of promise and gaiety.

Of friends and a mama who loved her. Her position at the great house with the dowager Lady Carr. The hope of a Season when her mama had written to Lady Kemsley, and she had agreed to sponsor her. How life could change in but a moment.

"As you are aware, I worked in Lord Carr's estate. I read to his grandmother most days and kept her company. I earned a little stipend for this service, and I supposed you could call me a lady's companion. She was a lovely woman, and I grew fond of her and her toward me, although I never wanted anything more from that family than the little payment I earned. I never looked to Lord Carr as a potential suitor. There was something about him that I had never liked, not even as a boy. He would often come into the village and lord it all over us that he was to be the future viscount, and we would be his people as if he were the king."

Henry leaned back in his chair and clasped the sides of his seat. Sophie noted his white knuckles but continued, needing him to know.

"A week before my sixteenth birthday, the now late Lord Carr announced the betrothal of his eighteen-year-old son to Lady Fanny Montfoot. His grandmother was overjoyed, and because she liked my company so much, I was invited to attend the betrothal ball as a guest to celebrate. I had never been to a ball at the great house. As Mama was in discussions with Harlow regarding sponsoring me for a Season, a society ball before I came of age seemed the perfect opportunity to practice my dancing and social discourse."

Sophie glanced out the library window, the inky night suiting the somber mood of the room. She closed her eyes, hating Lord Carr with every fiber of her body.

"I attended the ball in my favorite dress, nothing smart, I grant you. In fact, the hem was stained by the time I arrived because I had to walk. Nevertheless, Mama had put some flowers in my hair, and I thought I looked appropriate. The night was interesting. Many people spoke to me due to being near the dowager Lady Carr, and I even danced with a gentleman or two. But as all things must, the ball came to an end, and I started home. Most of the guests were staying at the estate for the evening, and my walk back to the village was one I had made numerous times during the day, so I was not worried about making it at night. It was scarcely twenty minutes from the village."

Henry cleared his throat and adjusted his seat. Sophie met his eyes, the white pallor of his face making her heart race.

"I did not know it, but the now Lord Carr followed me and caught up to me near the gates of his father's estate. He offered to escort me home, and I thought what a lovely gesture for him to offer such a service. I did not know that he had far more nefarious ideas for the reason he walked me back to the village."

"Sophie ..." Henry breathed, and she knew he could guess where her account was headed.

"Out of nowhere, he asked me to stop, and without warning, he shoved me to the ground. I tried to get up and run, but he came down atop me, and I could not move. He was so heavy and strong, so much stronger than I thought he would be. He hit me several times, and ..." She closed her eyes, recalling the pain, his hand about her throat. "I thought he was going to kill me, Henry. I stopped fighting and pretended to be somewhere else. I closed my eyes and thought of home, of my cat, my mama who needed me, of the future I wanted for myself, and I refused to allow him to take that too. So I relented, I gave him what he wanted, and I survived." Sophie wiped at her cheeks, hating that Lord Carr had made her cry once more, something she had promised never to do again.

"Lord Carr took everything from me that night. The last card I had to play that made me eligible to believe I could find a loving husband in London. I thought all of that was gone, but Mama helped me, we prayed no child came of the rape, and it did not. Lord Carr went on an extended honeymoon abroad, and I kept myself busy with etiquette lessons at home, safe and away from any possible scandal like the one I avoided by sheer luck. I had not seen his lordship until this Season. He has boasted to me, ridiculed me all Season, and blackmailed us both. But I cannot let him win. I will not be seen to be the one at fault. To give him such power means I lose, and I cannot survive if that happens."

She jerked as strong arms lifted her from the chair and pulled her into a comforting embrace. He held her tight, almost uncomfortably close, but did not relent.

"No, my love, my darling Sophie. It is I who is sorry. Not you. Never you, not for this. You did not ask for what he did. He is the one who ought to be ashamed, not you."

Sophie met his eyes and could see the pleading light, the honesty of his words shining back at her. "You believe me?"

He wrenched her close again. "I believe you. Please forgive me for being such a bastard. If you hate me now, I would understand why."

She studied him a moment, pausing to debate his words. "I could never hate you, Henry. I may have been mad and disappointed, but nothing harsher than that," she said. "I love you. I want a life with you, a future, not to dwell in my past."

He smiled, the first she had seen in far too long. "I want that too."

THIRTY-ONE

However, Sophie wasn't ready quite yet to forgive him entirely. "But there is one other matter that concerns me that we're yet to discuss. What of this bet? I think it is your turn to explain, is it not?" Sophie said.

And she was right. He needed to explain what had happened and why he had done such a foolish thing. A mistake he would never make again.

"A mistake I tried to correct and could not." He walked her over to the settee and sat them down. "I arrived in London, and within a day of being here, rumors began of my conquests of the fairer sex. I fled to Whites, one place mamas of the *ton* did not throw their daughters at my head. As one does, I glanced curiously at the betting book." At Sophie's frown, he raised his hands in submission. "Granted, the betting book should not be allowed, but that is not my choice to make. But this evening, there was a bet regarding you, and without thought, I scribbled down my name."

"What did the bet say exactly?" she asked, needing to hear it from Henry.

He thought back to it, wanting to be as truthful as she had been. "Nothing of consequence, merely asked the gentlemen to put their names down for those who wished to court you and see who won your favor. I should never have put my name to that, for I did not even know you then. But upon meeting you, I knew my mistake, and I could only hope you would never learn of it."

"And yet I did," she stated, not giving way to how or what she was thinking.

"And I knew if you should be so unfortunate, you would question my affection for you, which is not what I wanted. I fell in love with you, not because I could win one thousand pounds, but because I love everything about you. You're one of the dearest people I have ever met. Passionate and funny, and loyal. I could not ask for more in my wife. I feel honored and blessed to have met you and never wish to be parted from you again."

"And you thought I would judge you if I found out you had put your name to a bet regarding me?"

He nodded, although the sound of such an

outcome now sounded absurd when she said it. "I did initially come and speak to you because I had put my name to the betting book, but the moment we met, all of that paled into insignificance. I wanted to know you, dance, and spend time with you, and no blunt would ever alter that fact."

She reached up and clasped his cheeks in her hands. "I believe you, Henry. I suppose I'm just a little hurt that I was only worth a thousand pounds." She said, making light of the situation, but he could not. She was not a jest, and he did not want her to think she ever was.

"I'm so sorry for how I reacted to hearing Lord Carr's words. I ought to have stood beside you and listened to you, but shamefully I was ashamed. No, that is not the right word. I was embarrassed. I thought I had professed everything to you and shared my secrets, and your responses were a lie. I pretended to live up to the *ton's* expectations for so long. Henry James, the future Duke of Holland, was just like his father. A rakehell of the wildest order, and yet I was not. I had never been with a woman before you, and then to hear that you had been intimate with Lord Carr, my mind bolted to the worst possible conclusion it could imagine at the time.

"I thought you gave yourself willingly to him. That you had affections for this man in the past, and he broke your heart, which in turn drove me to loathe him. I wish that were the case now. I wish you had loved him and given yourself to him because knowing what did occur to you is far worse than I could have envisioned. I want to annihilate the man for his actions. I cannot bear to think of the fear you felt."

"Henry," she sighed, hugging him, holding him when it was not he who needed reassuring and comforting but she. He held her tight, wishing he could change the past few weeks but knowing that although he could not, he could make their future much better than their past.

"I love you so very much, Sophie," he declared. "Please forgive me for being such a prig and arse and any other insults you can throw at my head."

She pulled away and smiled. "I have already said I forgive you. There is no other choice for me but to do so, but please do not ever shut me out if we disagree. I could not bear it a second time."

"I will never do so again. I promise on my life that I shall not."

He lost himself in her eyes and could not thank the gods enough that she was back in his arms. That everything was right in the world.

"Make love to me, Henry," she asked him, and his knees almost buckled at how hastily he stood and scooped her up in his arms before starting for the door.

· · ·

SOPHIE LAUGHED AS HENRY STRUGGLED with her in his arms up the vast staircase before making his way down the long passageway to his room. With his labored breathing, she bit back a retort that perhaps they ought to waylay their re-union until he had caught his breath.

Upon making the suite of rooms, he threw off his jacket, wrenching his shirt free of his breeches and throwing it aside.

Sophie worked quickly on the buttons at the back of her dress and forgot about taking their time. The sight of her virile husband, his eyes burning with desire, with love, was too much to ignore. "Help me with the high hooks," she asked, giving him her back.

He all but ripped them open before untying the ribbons on her stays. The dress and stays dropped to her feet, and she reached for the hem of the shift, sliding it over her head.

Sophie bit her lip, naked before Henry except for the silk stockings and lace slippers she still wore.

"You look utterly delectable," he said, his voice reverberating with need, his gaze sliding over her like a caress. A shiver stole down her spine at the expectation of being with him again.

Henry kicked off his boots and breeches be-fore she sauntered over to him in the most sen-sual manner she could summon and pushed against his chest, tumbling him onto the bed.

His smile warmed her soul before she inched onto the soft mattress, crawling over to straddle him. The feel of skin on skin, his scratchy chest hair tickling her breasts, made need simmer and burn.

"I've missed this," she admitted, kissing him, his cheeks, his neck before biting the lobe of his ear. "I'm going to enjoy having you again, husband."

Sophie positioned herself over him and lowered herself onto his rigid manhood. They groaned, satisfaction licking down her spine as he filled her, claimed her once more. His strong hands clasped her hips, and he thrust deep and long into her core.

"Yes, Sophie," he gasped, watching her with hooded eyes. "You feel so good."

Her body rose and fell, taking, stroking, and working them both toward climax. Without warning, Henry flipped her onto her back, thrusting hard, taking her with a determination she had never experienced before but liked quite a lot.

Tonight was like making love for the first time, except now there were no secrets, no scandals, and lies between them. They had bared their souls and told all there was to know. Now their future could commence in earnest.

No one could come between them. Nothing could rip them apart, not ever.

"I love you," he whispered against her lips, taking her mouth in a searing kiss before she could answer. Sophie wrapped her legs about his hips, holding him, needing him like her body required air. He was her life, her husband, and heart.

The first tremors of her release thrummed through her, and she let go, reveled in the feel of the pleasure that Henry gifted her. "Henry," she moaned as her body came apart in his arms. Shattered into a million pieces that only he could put together again.

He groaned her name into her ear, loving that she could make a virile, powerful man crumble in her arms.

They stayed locked together for some time before he slumped beside her, pulling her into his arms. "You are never to leave my bed again," he ordered her.

She nodded, snuggling up to his side. "I do not ever intend to. You're my duke."

He smiled, contentment he had not felt for weeks making his eyes grow heavy. "I would not have it any other way, Duchess."

Epilogue

S everal days later, Henry sat at the breakfast table, his appetite ravenous after his delectable night with his wife. He grinned, unable to hide the satisfaction and amusement that being married to Sophie brought forth in him.

He was the luckiest man alive, and no one could tell him otherwise.

His beautiful duchess entered the room, and a pang of alarm went off in his head at the shadows beneath her eyes. This evening he would allow her to sleep peacefully without any conjugal activities. Without a care for who was present, she kissed him good morning and sat at his side.

A footman poured her a cup of tea and placed toast before her, her usual breakfast he had not seen her deviate from since he'd returned home.

"Is everything well, my dear?" he asked her.

She nodded, sipping her tea and bringing a little of the color back to her cheeks. "I am well, thank you. Just a little tired, that is all." She bit into her toast

He periodically checked on her, not entirely sure she was telling the truth. Her masticating of the toast appeared slow and with little enthusiasm. "Are you certain you are well, my love?"

Sophie picked up her tea and sipped. "Certainly, and I'm about to be picked up by Lady Hervey. We're to Bond Street this morning. She's sponsoring her husband's younger twin sisters next Season and thought I might be able to help her since I'm familiar with the process. I said that I would. I hope you do not mind."

"Not at all," he said, glad she was making friends and enjoying London and what was left of the Season. "When did you meet Lady Hervey?" he asked.

"Before our wedding, we had chatted at a couple of events. She's of similar age to me and is friends with everyone we know."

Henry smiled, feeling for the first time a notion of contentment they had not had before. Since they had repaired the damage that Lord Carr had driven between them, the past several days had been incredible, and each day he marveled at how lucky he was that Sophie was his wife.

Sophie set her teacup down. "Please leave us," she ordered the footmen, who did as she asked and left them alone, closing the door behind them. Henry glanced up, curious. "Was there something you wished to say in private?"

She slipped from her chair and came to stand beside him. He chuckled when she sat in his lap, wrapping her arms around his neck. "No, I just wanted some time in your arms before I leave for the day. I believe we're to have lunch at the countess's house. I shall not see you until this evening."

"I shall miss you too." And he would. He had grown so used to having Sophie with him most hours of every day that, at times, he wondered what he did before they were married. How tiresome and lonesome life had been then.

"I shall miss you more," she replied, stealing a kiss.

One would never be enough, and he clasped her cheek, bringing her back for more. Hunger and need tore through him and one that she did not try to bank.

She kissed him back, and his body roared to have her. Before he could think better of it or where they were, he pushed the dishes aside on the table and slipped Sophie onto it, stepping between her legs.

He gathered up her gown, running his hand

against her wet mons. She threw back her head and moaned, reveling in his touch.

"I want you," he said, his voice hoarse.

"Yes," she agreed, but he could not. She was about to go shopping, and his having her would delay her day out, and she deserved a lovely jaunt with friends. But nor could he deny them what they both wanted. It would not hurt her friend to wait five more minutes.

He sat back on the chair, and she threw him a curious look before he pushed against her stomach. "Lie down, Sophie. I have not finished my breakfast."

She bit her lip, her eyes flaring wide at his meaning before she did as he asked, giving herself to him without argument. His need meant he did not dally but went straight to her mons. He licked the sweet nectar between her legs, paying homage to her nubbin that soon begged for attention.

She was wet, and he delved his tongue along her weeping lips, the sound of her pleasure, her enjoyment, music to his ears.

He entered her with his fingers, teasing her from within, and she squirmed. Her hands clasped the hair on his head, directing him, grinding his mouth where she liked it most.

His name slipped from her lips as he felt the first tremors of her release. She rode his hand as he fucked her notch with his tongue, wringing every ounce of satisfaction he could.

She lay on the table for a moment or two, bare and open to his gaze. The most perfect view in all of London, he was sure.

She held out her hand, and he helped her to sit up, settling her dress about her legs. The smile on his lips could not be tamed.

"Well, if I were not awake before, I certainly am now," she teased, sitting on his lap again. "You are as wicked as you are good," she said.

"Think of me when you're out today, and I shall do the same."

She kissed the tip of his nose and stood.

"What are you purchasing today, my love? Surely it is not more gowns."

A knowing light entered her eyes as she went and stood before the mirror hanging above the fireplace and adjusted her hair. "Nothing in particular, but I do wish to buy some clothing for the nursery, new blankets, and order some toys. Small items such as those."

Henry's heart froze, and he stood, his chair scraping the parquetry floor and making a go-dawful sound. "Wh-what did you say?" His mouth gaped, and he closed it, the thoughts in his mind moving a million times too fast.

"For the baby we're going to have, my darling," she said, glancing over her shoulder, her smile as joyful as his.

He closed the space between them, reaching for her hands. "You're going to have a baby? We're going to have a baby?" The words were foreign, but wonderful too.

She nodded, tears welling in her eyes. "Are you happy?"

Henry wrenched her into his arms, promising never to let her go, never to let anything happen to her. "It is wonderful news, my love. A child, our child, well, you have made me the happiest of men." He could not believe the news. He was going to be a father.

She clasped his face, chuckling. "Can you imagine a little Lord or Lady running about our home? I cannot wait to meet the baby."

He marveled at her, unable to comprehend how happy one man could be. "Boy or girl, they will be loved equally. I'm so happy, Sophie. I love you so." He could not stop hugging her. In fact, he was unsure if he would ever be able to stop. Not that she seemed to care.

"I love you too, Henry." She stepped out of his arms. "But now I must go shopping. I have a baby to prepare for."

"Mayhap it would be best if I accompany you, my love. I do not want you carrying anything heavy. We must take better care of you," he said, remembering their escapades on the table, not to mention this morning in bed.

Damn it all to hell, he was a rogue who needed to allow his expectant wife to rest.

She chuckled and started for the door. "Best grab your coat and hat then, Your Grace. The carriage waits for no one," she teased.

He followed close on her heels, unsure he would ever be doing anything different for the rest of their splendid life.

Not that he would have it any other way.

Dear Reader

Thank you for taking the time to read *A Wager with a Duke*! I hope you enjoyed the first book in The Wayward Yorks, a spin-off series to the bestselling The Wayward Woodvilles.

I'm so thankful for my readers and their support. If you're able, I would appreciate an honest review of *A Wager with a Duke*. As they say, feed an author, leave a review!

Alternatively, you can keep in contact with me by visiting my website www.-tamaragill.com or following me online.

Don't Miss Tamara's Other Romance Series

The Wayward Yorks

A Wager with a Duke

My Reformed Rogue

Wild, Wild, Duke

The Wayward Woodvilles

A Duke of a Time

On a Wild Duke Chase

Speak of the Duke

Every Duke has a Silver Lining

One Day my Duke Will Come

Surrender to the Duke

My Reckless Earl

Brazen Rogue

The Notorious Lord Sin

Wicked in My Bed

League of Unweddable Gentlemen

Tempt Me, Your Grace

Hellion at Heart

Dare to be Scandalous

To Be Wicked With You
Kiss Me, Duke
The Marquess is Mine

Kiss the Wallflower
A Midsummer Kiss
A Kiss at Mistletoe
A Kiss in Spring
To Fall For a Kiss
A Duke's Wild Kiss
To Kiss a Highland Rose

To Marry a Rogue
Only an Earl Will Do
Only a Duke Will Do
Only a Viscount Will Do
Only a Marquess Will Do
Only a Lady Will Do

Lords of London
To Bedevil a Duke
To Madden a Marquess
To Tempt an Earl
To Vex a Viscount
To Dare a Duchess

To Marry a Marchioness

Royal House of Atharia

To Dream of You

A Royal Proposition

Forever My Princess

A Time Traveler's Highland Love

To Conquer a Scot

To Save a Savage Scot

To Win a Highland Scot

A Stolen Season

A Stolen Season

A Stolen Season: Bath

A Stolen Season: London

Scandalous London

A Gentleman's Promise

A Captain's Order

A Marriage Made in Mayfair

High Seas & High Stakes

His Lady Smuggler

Her Gentleman Pirate

A Wallflower's Christmas Wreath

Daughters Of The Gods

Banished

Guardian

Fallen

Stand Alone Books

Defiant Surrender

A Brazen Agreement

To Sin with Scandal

Outlaws

About the Author

Tamara is an Australian author who grew up in an old mining town in country South Australia, where her love of history was founded. So much so, she made her darling husband travel to the UK for their honeymoon, where she dragged him from one historical monument and castle to another.

A mother of three, her two little gentlemen in the making, a future lady (she hopes) keep her busy in the real world, but whenever she gets a moment's peace she loves to write romance novels in an array of genres, including regency, medieval and time travel.